Aisha Alaskar is, as of yet, a rookie when it comes to writing novels, but she won't let that stop her. Currently, she lives with her family in the UAE, giving new hobbies a try every now and then. She is doing her best to balance writing and being a student, as she works on the sequel to the *Wars of Life* three-book series. She plans to write several more books in the coming years, for this has grown into much more than just a hobby.

For everyone who knew of my dream to become a writer and helped me find the correct path to the center of this maze of words.

Aisha Alaskar

WARS OF LIFE GARY

AUSTIN MACAULEY PUBLISHERS™
LONDON • CAMBRIDGE • NEW YORK • SHARJAH

Copyright © Aisha Alaskar 2022

The right of Aisha Alaskar to be identified as author of this work has been asserted by the author in accordance with Federal Law No. (7) of UAE, Year 2002, Concerning Copyrights and Neighboring Rights.

All rights reserved. No part of this publication may be reproduced, stored in a retrieval system, or transmitted in any form or by any means, electronic, mechanical, photocopying, recording, or otherwise, without the prior permission of the publishers.

Any person who commits any unauthorized act in relation to this publication may be liable to legal prosecution and civil claims for damages.

This is a work of fiction. Names, characters, businesses, places, events, locales, and incidents are either the products of the author's imagination or used in a fictitious manner. Any resemblance to actual persons, living or dead, or actual events is purely coincidental.

ISBN – 9789948044918 – (Paperback)
ISBN – 9789948044925 – (E-Book)

Application Number: MC-10-01-8579241
Age Classification: 17+

The age group that matches the content of the books has been classified according to the age classification system issued by the Ministry of Culture and Youth.

Printer Name: iPrint Global Ltd
Printer Address: Witchford, England

First Published 2022
AUSTIN MACAULEY PUBLISHERS FZE
Sharjah Publishing City
P.O Box [519201]
Sharjah, UAE
www.austinmacauley.ae
+971 655 95 202

Thank you:

To my best friends Asma, Amna, and Maha for helping me write this novel and for motivating me when I would lose hope.

To my parents and family for supporting, motivating, and listening to me each time I talked about this story.

To my teachers for teaching me everything I needed to know to accomplish my dream and for giving me new ideas.

To anyone who reads this novel for being patient with the storyline. I hope you continue to read the whole series.

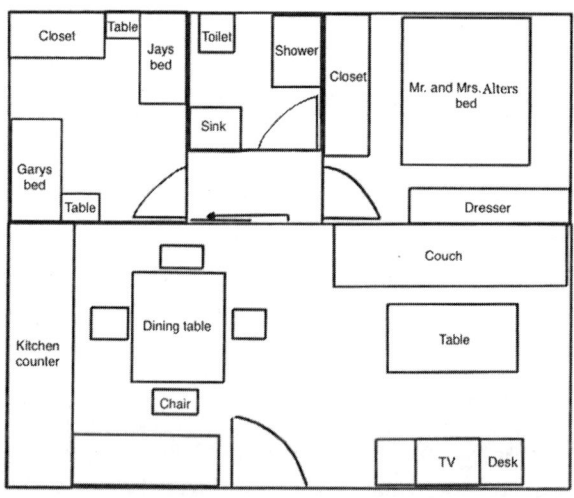

Chapter 1
Mysterious Brother

The Alter family are a long line of criminals, raising their children to be the same. The eldest of the three brothers carrying the Alter name Kyle died in a car accident; he was at fault. Dealing with drugs while driving past a red light didn't end so well. The third and youngest brother, Liam, was caught red-handed after an attempted murder and was imprisoned. The middle brother, Michael, on the other hand, married and had two kids, Jay and Gary.

Michael's wife, Lola Sligmen, adored her first-born's unique look, for he had inherited her eyes, or one eye had, while the other had inherited his grandfather's eyes, Lola's father. Although Lola didn't look like it, she loved gambling, and her family resented her for it. "Such women like you should not waste their time on games such as these!" they said. In the end Lola's mother threw her out of the house. That's when Lola, stubborn as she is, went out gambling again.

After a good game with Michael and a little opening up to him, he invited her over to take shelter for a couple of days till things cooled down with her family, but her mother never forgave her. After a few months, they ended up married.

Jay, Lola and Michael's first-born son, had one delicate blue left eye, just like his mother's, and a black right eye, just like his grandfather's. Jay's hair was the same color as his right eye, pitch black. With the handsome face Jay had and his lightly tanned skin, he was a perfectly cute son.

Gary, the second son to come across the Alter family, was as handsome as his brother. With straw blond hair, delicate blue eyes, and pale skin, he looked like a harmless sketch, all silent and still.

Even though the Alters had such beautiful kids, they did not care for them much. After entering preschool, Mr. and Mrs. Alter would teach them the ways of taking care of the house: cleaning, organizing, going to the grocery store to buy essential items, and even a bit of cooking. By the time they've learned everything, the boys would be the ones in charge of the house. Every day after school they would come home and start on their chores. When the Alter couple was in a bad mood, they would take it upon themselves to abuse the two boys.

Mr. and Mrs. Alter were the most relaxed people around the city, using their own children as servants. The brothers, on the other hand, would keep each other company, for they didn't get the chance to experience much fun as most kids around their age would. This affected each of the brothers differently. Jay became a socially strong and brave boy that would sacrifice anything for the people he loved. Gary turned out as helpful as a first-aid kit; he would help cure the wounds of the people he loved and took care of them during hard times and would listen to their complaints. However, Gary did not turn out as social as his brother, nor as strong; he was more fragile and weak.

After school the brothers would stop by the library to waste time and finish their homework in a place that would have all the resources they needed. Some days they were joined by Jay's friends, Daniel Higgins, Fred Walter, and Heath Aberman. Fred was the only one of Jay's friends that knew about their parents and what the brothers go through at home, but he had sworn to keep it secret.

After coming home late one day, the boys found their parents yet again gambling with their friends over. As soon as they opened the door, Mr. Alter stood up and started shouting. "Where in the world have you been? Do you know how long it will take you to finish everything? And don't you dare go to bed without finishing your work! Go get us some drinks. Don't just stand there, go!"

"Come on, Michael, they're just kids," said one of the men sitting around the table. This person was dark-skinned and very tall, with little hair. He was a new guest that hadn't been there before. "How old are they?"

Mrs. Alter looked at her sons and said, "The big one's 8 and the small one's 6." Looking at them both right in the eyes, she added, "They're old enough to have jobs and they're still in the house."

"Does she even know her own age?" whispered Jay into Gary's ear. They both turned to the kitchen with a grin.

After they finished making dinner, mashed potatoes, cooked vegetables, and the meat that their mother had prepared, their parents were still gambling. It was 10 o'clock and the brothers finally finished their chores, but their parents were still gambling, and Mr. Alter seemed like the one with the biggest pile of money by his side. The boys went to bed, sliding the door shut in the hallway. They each changed into their nightclothes and prepared themselves for the following day.

Creak.

Gary lifted his head and look at the bedroom door. Jay was leaning against it with a shocked and worried look on his face.

"What are you... What happened?"

Jay suddenly looked up as though he finally realized where he was. "Bathroom. I went to the bathroom, go back to sleep."

Gary looked back at the door after Jay laid down in his bed. It sounded like his parents were still gambling. They were arguing about something, then suddenly Mr. Alter's voice came strong enough to travel clearly through the closed door.

"Fine! You win, alright? You'll have it next week!"

Jay curled up in his bed, pulling the sheets over his head, and the place went silent again. Gary put his head back on the pillow and, looking at his brother's motionless figure, fell asleep.

Walking to school the next day was a quiet trip. Gary kept looking from Jay to the ground. Finally he pulled up the courage and asked, "Jay, about last night...what really happened? Did Dad do something to you?"

"Something like that," said Jay, without averting his eyes from the road or stopping in his tracks.

Gary sat down on the same bench he always occupied at lunch. He wasn't even halfway through lunch when Fred came to visit with a mouthful of questions.

"Hey Gary! Do you know what's up with Jay? He isn't talking and I know something's wrong! Is it your parents?"

"Quiet down a bit, Fred," said Gary, looking around. "I don't know. Ever since last night, he's been acting weird and I mean weirder than normal."

"So it isn't your parents?" whispered Fred.

"I don't know what it is, but it looks like he has his mind on it. Maybe it's something good," decided Gary, returning to his lunch. If it really was something that their father lost in a bet, it didn't matter. The only mystery was why they were keeping that thing for one more week? Did they need to fix it or prepare it?

Going to the library after school was also a quiet trip which Fred decided to join. Jay finished up his work and took out a book to read silently while Fred kept trying to start a conversation but getting no response. When Gary finished his homework, Jay stood up and said, "Let's go back home."

Ignoring Fred, Jay walked away. Gary waved sadly to Fred and ran after Jay.

The next day and the day after were the same. On the third day when Jay and Gary were washing the dishes, Jay froze, staring at the wall ahead. When Gary poked him on the shoulder, Jay jumped and dropped the plate in his hand.

Smash!

"What did you punks do?" Mr. Alter had gotten to his feet. "You're paying for that!" he continued as he slapped Jay across the face.

Jay stomped away and came back with the red-and-blue box that he used to store his coins in. Pushing it against his father's stomach and letting it fall to the ground, he said, "I don't need any money anyway."

"Fine! You're not getting any more! Both of you!" shouted Mr. Alter, picking up the box and going back to the couch to count the coins inside the box.

The next day, Monday, Mrs. Alter spilled some juice in the master bedroom and called Gary to clean the mess. Jay stopped what he was doing and went to get a towel. Gary snatched the towel out of Jay's hand, saying, "Let me do it, you don't have to!"

"Gary please, I want to do it." Jay snatched the towel back and went to his parents' bedroom.

Gary, staring after his brother, overheard his parents debating what to do with their money supply. *Since when did Jay like or want to work?*

Gary was fading in and out of sleep worried about Jay. He rolled over to find Jay in a sweater, jeans, and running shoes looking at him to see if he was up. Gary sat up on his bed, rubbed his eyes, and said, "What are you doing in the middle of the night?"

Jay didn't respond but turned his head around and continued what he was doing. Gary looked at Jay and frowned. Knowing something is different but not being able to tell what is annoying!

Gary got up out of bed and sat down next to Jay. A big pile of cash was sitting next to Jay's backpack which now was filled with clothes, a notebook, his pencil case, a toothbrush, and toothpaste in a plastic bag, and a big water bottle.

"Are you running away?"

Jay had joked about running away before, but he never really meant it. "Please Gary, go back to sleep."

"Where did you get all this money?" Gary couldn't sleep now, his heart was beating too hard to rest.

"Umm... I saw the password to Mom and Dad's safe when I was cleaning the floor."

"You can't go! What about our promise?!"

Jay froze, remembering their promise.

*

A few year back, the brothers had been punished for telling one of their friends, Fred, where they lived. They were spanked on the hands with a wooden stick that their father had bought especially for when he needed to teach them a lesson.

In their room later that night, Gary couldn't sleep. He was crying into his pillow when he felt a slight smack on his head. Jay had flicked his finger at Gary's head, hitting him.

"Be quiet, I want to sleep."

"It hurts!"

"I know." Jay had been hiding his tears from his parents. He hadn't cried when his father hit him harder and even more than Gary because of it. Now his eyes were full of tears ready to burst. No one other than Gary saw Jay's tears. "Don't ever leave me, Jay!" Gary hugged his brother.

Gary wanted to be like Jay, he wanted to be brave. Apparently even the brave cried, Jay had silent tears flowing down his cheeks.

"We'll always be brothers. We'll always look out for each other, like a team of heroes, each one watching the back of the other. Promise?" Jay embarrassed himself by saying such a silly thing, but he was scared of his father.

"Promise!"

"Forever right?"

"Forever!" Gary had already been prepared to accept the promise because he wanted the same himself.

"If only it wasn't the last day of school, Dad wouldn't have hit us like that," Jay added in anger.

*

Jay went quiet, he couldn't say anything against that. "Jay, please! Tell me what going on!"

"I—I can't."

"Please!"

"It's not that—"

"Jay!"

"This is bigger than life or death!" That anger came out of nowhere.

"Wh-what do you mean?"

"I don't know what it is exactly! I might die if I stay here. So let me go!"

Jay stuffed the money in his bag, zipped it closed, and opened the window above his bedside table. Climbing out of it, he said, "If Mom and Dad ask where I am, pretend you don't know."

"Can't I come with you?" Gary was scared, he didn't want to be alone.

"I thought of that too. At first I thought it would be a good idea, but it's too dangerous for you. It would be better if you stay here with Mom and Dad."

Gary didn't want to believe that. "But can I at least run away too? You don't have to look after me!" Tears were flowing down Gary's cheeks.

"Gary...I'm sorry." Jay jumped out of the window and stretched his hand up to close it. He couldn't bear hearing his brother's voice before leaving. He felt like he was leaving a big chunk of himself behind.

Gary ran across the room and jumped on his bed. *This is all a bad dream! I'll open my eyes and Jay will be in his bed snoring! I won't be alone! I'll have Jay!* Gary kept crying in his bed until he fell asleep.

The next day when Gary was eating breakfast trying to look as normal as ever, his mother came up to him and asked, "Where's Jay?"

"In the bathroom."

"No, he's not, I was just in there."

Gary pasted a confused look on his face and turned to look at the bathroom.

"Lola!" It sounded like someone had just shredded all the valuable stuff in the house. Mr. Alter was furious. "What did you do to the money?!"

"What?!" That got Mrs. Alter's attention.

As soon as she left the room, Gary bolted out of the house. After running down a few blocks, Gary slowed down. Waiting for him at the school gates was none other than Fred.

"Where's Jay?" Fred asked.

"Go away!"

"What?!"

"I said go away!"

"Did they do something to him?"

"Just leave me alone!" said Gary, stomping his foot on the ground. Gary knew it was pretty childish but he was a child and Gary wanted to get away as soon as possible, he wanted to forget about Jay's situation.

Fred kept watch over Gary that day, but he did not try to talk to him again.

When Gary got home carrying his bag in his hands, he opened the door to see the dark-skinned guy sitting on the couch.

A hand suddenly closed the door, picked Gary up by the neck of his shirt, and pushed him against the door. Gary's hand let go of the bag and wrapped around his father's arms.

"Where is he?"

Mr. Alter looked murderous. Gary started crying, it hurt to be pressed against a wooden door.

"I do-don't know!"

Mr. Alter shook Gary and repeated his question, "Where is Jay?!"

"He ran away!"

Mr. Alter threw Gary to the ground and kicked him aside violently. Gary got up and, against the pain, walked to his bedroom crying. Closing the door, he heard the three adults arguing outside. Was he going to be killed now?

A couple of weeks passed and Jay was still not heard of. Mr. and Mrs. Alter had started arguing loudly. Fred hadn't talked to Gary after the incident and he had, by the looks of it, forgotten about Jay. Gary continued to visit the library after school; it protected him from his parents for a little while.

Chapter 2
Following the Path
of One's Ancestors

Four weeks had passed and the parents were still arguing. Every time Gary's mother got angry, she would come and beat him up.

After a long fight, Mrs. Alter stomped into the boys' room and started shouting undecipherable words. Gary was getting ready to go to bed when she walked up to him and told him that it was all his fault. Mrs. Alter slapped the child and continued to abuse him while repeating the same sentence again and again. "All your fault!"

A few days later, Gary was putting the last of the dishes away when he overheard his mother shouting at Mr. Alter.

"UGH! JUST KILL ME THEN!"

Mr. Alter came storming into the kitchen, opened a drawer, pulled out a knife, and walked back to the room, slamming the drawer shut behind him. Gary took the fire extinguisher off of the kitchen counter and ran after his father in his panic.

"Dad, no! Don't!"

Gary pulled out the pin, but it was too late. The door swung open after a shriek filled the air. Mr. Alter had his hand wrapped around the knife deep in Mrs. Alter's stomach.

"Go away!" screamed Gary in a shrieking voice while pushing on the lever and spraying a foaming substance on his father.

Mr. Alter suddenly turned to Gary and started walking towards him.

Gary dropped the fire extinguisher and backed away shakily. "Ge-get away! No—back! Murderer!"

Murderer? That was what had made Mr. Alter realize what he just did. He stopped in his tracks and looked at his hands. He was stained with blood and foam. He looked back at his wife now silently weeping on the floor next to the bed with a knife sticking out of her stomach.

"This is all your fault!" Mr. Alter spat at the dying woman on the ground. Ignoring Gary completely, he ran out of the room and out of the house.

Gary got up breathing heavily as he walked to his moaning mother. He sat down, staring at the knife. *I should pull it out, shouldn't I?* he thought. He reached out with his hand and touched the knife's handle when his mother twitched and moaned. Eyes filling with tears, he placed his second hand on the wound, next to the knife. He pulled the knife lightly.

"Ugh, don't—don't!"

"Mom…" Gary let go of the knife and held his hands to his chest. He didn't know what to do now.

"Help! Gar…he—I… I love y-you, Gary, h-help me…" She was losing consciousness slowly.

How dare she, how dare she say that she loves me when she needs help from me! Why didn't she say that when Jay ran away! I'll never forgive her!

"I hate you!" Gary shouted as the tears he was holding back burst forth.

Without looking at her face, Gary rushed out of the room, leaving the door half open and hurried to the telephone, picked it up, and stopped. What should he do? His parents never let him use the phone before, how was he going to call the police? How was he going to call an ambulance?

His grip loosened and the phone fell out of his small hands.

The phone was held inches off the ground by the cable. Gary wiped the tears off his face and walked to his bedroom without realizing what he's doing. He laid down on the bed face up and squeezed the blanket as his hands formed fists. He suddenly felt the urge to fall asleep.

*

Gary had just woken up. He got out of bed and went to the bathroom to wash his face, ignoring the half open door to his parents' bedroom.

After getting ready to go to school, he picked up his bag and opened the front door.

Gary spotted Fred next to the school entrance.

"Hi Fred," he said without considering the fact that he hadn't talked to Fred for the past month.

"Uhh. Hi, I guess..." Fred was confused, Mr. Ryan had told Fred to watch Gary but keep his distance at the same time. What could possibly make Gary forget about what happened?

Fred continued to stare at Gary and realized how he was as white as a sheet of paper, his eyes were ghostly, and his lips were dry and pale.

"I need to use the restroom." Fred told Daniel and Heath, then got up and headed straight to the staffroom.

He spotted Mr. Ryan in the crowd of teachers. He stopped beside him and said, "Mr. Ryan?"

The tall teacher turned around and smiled at the sight of his favorite student.

"Hello Fred."

"It's about Gary again."

"What happened?"

"He's different. He looks like a ghost, and he talked to me! I just wanna make sure nothing bad happened to him, and about Jay, I still think we should tell somebody. We can't just keep pretending he went to another school. I really don't think we should ignore this and if we could at least—"

"Slow down a bit. Going to their house would just be too dangerous. It might get them in trouble."

"I don't care! I want to go to their house!"

A few teachers turned around at this loud statement.

"You don't really mean that, do you? I'm almost done getting things ready with child services, but seeing as you're this desperate, how about we check on them, huh, will that calm you down?"

"Okay, I'll tell them I needed my pencil back from Gary. They'll have to let me in."

As planned Fred and Mr. Ryan visited the Alter house after school. Gary didn't go to the library today. Fred knew this after following him with Mr. Ryan—his favorite teacher.

Knock, knock, knock.

Gary opened the door and was surprised to see Fred outside.

"Uh, Gary! I forgot m-my favorite pencil! I mean, I lent it to Jay and just remembered about it. Can I come in?"

"Sure, Jay's asleep so try not to wake him up, okay?"

"Okay."

Gary showed Fred the way to his bedroom. "Where are your parents?"

"They went out."

Fred looked at Gary's bed, then at Jay's. "Where's Jay? You said he was sleeping."

Gary kept quiet as if he never heard Fred speak. Fred looked around not knowing what to do now. He spotted something on Gary's bed and went closer to see what it was. He gasped, turned, and stared at Gary, then suddenly ran out of the bedroom, across the living room, and out of the house. He faced the teacher waiting outside the door.

"It's—you gotta—just—"

"What's going on?!" Mr. Ryan was confused. "What happened inside there?"

"Blood!"

"What?!"

Mr. Ryan couldn't wait any longer. He approached the open door and entered the house. Gary stared at the teacher entering the house while he walked towards him. Fred, now standing at the front door, pointed to the left. Mr. Ryan, after looking back at Fred, walked into Gary's bedroom scanned the room, then walked closer to the bed in front of him. Looking at the blood-stained sheets, he turned and asked Gary, "Where did this blood come from?"

Gary's calm expression changed. He looked angry. "Go away." He had tears in his eyes now.

"Gary, I'm a—"

"Go away!" Gary raised his voice.

Mr. Ryan walked out of the bedroom and looked around. He entered the bathroom, scanned it, then turned to look at the master bedroom. He took a step closer to the bedroom when the tantrum began.

"No! GO AWAY! GO AWAY! AHHHHHHHHHH…"

Gary screamed, curled into a ball, and started crying. Then Fred ran forward and hugged him. He didn't know what else to do. He was scared, but Gary didn't push him away, instead he hugged him back.

Mr. Ryan opened the door and spotted the body on the floor. The foul rotting smell hit his nose with the force of a baseball bat. He closed the door before the boys could see what was inside.

"Come here." The teacher picked Gary up and held Fred's hand, then led them both to the living room and sat Gary on the couch, Fred sat next to him. He got up and called the police with the phone that was still hanging from the table. After he finished with the call, he turned to Gary, who had calmed down a little and kneeled down in front of him.

"Gary. I need you to tell me what happened because if you don't tell me, then the police will have to ask you about it."

After Gary calmed down enough to stop crying, he started to explain the situation.

"Jay ran away."

"What?"

"Let him explain, Fred," said Mr. Ryan.

"After that, Mom and Dad started fighting and then Mom made Dad angry, and he—I tried to stop him but the knife, and she—"

"That's enough, Gary, thank you."

After a couple of minutes, the police arrived and collected the body. Mr. Ryan told one of the policemen that was in a suit everything that Gary had told him. Then the man in the suit turned to Gary.

"So your brother ran away, huh?"

Gary didn't respond. "Can you tell me what he looked like?"

"His eyes, they are two different colors." Maybe the police could find him.

"Did they happen to be a blue and a black?"

Gary opened his eyes wide and nodded.

"I saw a boy like that one day. But I guess he ran away from us as well."

"Why did he run away from you?" Gary wanted to know everything. He hated but missed his big brother.

"I guess he didn't like us. We asked for his name and you know what he told us?"

Gary shook his head.

"He said his name was Gary! That must mean he's really thinking about you, huh?"

Gary didn't know how to take this. He turned away from the policeman to face his house. *Will Jay ever come back?*

Fred and his family allowed Gary to stay at their house after talking to the police. The incident was the main subject on the news the next day. They even put up a picture of both Gary and Jay, then asked the viewers to call the police if they ever see a boy that looked like Jay on the streets.

After talking about how the Alter couple had abused their kids, the reporter claimed that Mr. Alter had lived up to his family's name.

Not too long passed and the police requested Gary to tell them in detail everything that happened. They needed more information.

Chapter 3
Finding a New Family

The funeral was only a day away. Gary's black suit was in the closet. The police assigned a policeman to disguise as a guest to escort Gary there.

Gary had kept the funeral out of his mind the whole time, but now he had to face it head on. Gary didn't even know how to feel about this.

Gary felt sick whenever he woke up and found out he wasn't in his bedroom with Jay. He wanted his old life back. He would gladly pay the price of living as a servant for his parents once again. But now he had to sleep. *Tomorrow is going to be a very bad day,* he thought. After the funeral, Gary would meet his grandparents from his mother's side. He was going to live with them.

He woke up and looked up to see Fred standing near the doorway. "Come on, wake up. You're gonna be late," he said in a low, calm voice.

Scrambled eggs and toast were ready on the table. Breakfast was a silent meal. After that, Gary had to get dressed and meet the policeman at the door. Fred's mother gave him a hug before he left. Her red hair brushing against his cheek, he felt the welcoming warmth of a mother that he wanted now out of reach. Gary felt like crying in her arms, but he had to leave.

It was noisy. The guests were talking, some sitting on their seats, and waiting for the ceremony to begin. Gary was tired already. He felt a little too warm, everything and everyone was fuzzy in his eyes. He sat down with his escort and the ceremony started after a while of chitchat. The place fell silent. Everyone was sitting down and half of the hall was empty. Gary felt so dizzy he felt like a large bee was buzzing about. He could feel the policeman watching him and tried to keep a straight face.

When the ceremony ended, the policeman told Gary that his family was to meet him now and took him to a private room behind the ceremony hall. As soon as they entered the room, Gary fell to the ground. He was shaking now, he couldn't feel his body. He was exhausted.

He turned around and could barely see the outline of the policeman standing beside the door worried. He would come in and out of focus. The door opened again, and a small group of people entered the room. Gary's breath got heavy, he was trembling all over. *It's over*, he thought. *This is the end.* He saw flashes of gray and black, then someone came close enough to come into focus. Gary could see a black eye above his face. He pitied himself. Was he hallucinating Jay's eye before his death?

*

He was back home and he was sitting next to Jay in their bedroom. They were talking, their parents were asleep. They had the house to themselves so they went out to the kitchen and made some noodles. It was delicious and even more so with Jay.

*

He opened his eyes, it was dark. The roof seemed to stretch for miles above his head. There was a sleeping figure on the couch on the side of the cottage-sized room. He was a stranger, his head would rise only to fall back down.

Gary felt much better now. He was a new person and he had chosen to leave everything that happened behind. He got out of bed. He was starving as if he was grounded by his father. As soon as his foot touched the ground, he slid against the side of the bed to the floor. His legs ached, his whole body ached. He had no strength. How long had he been asleep?

There was a wheelchair next to his bed. He got up trembling and sat on the chair. Using his hands, he pushed the wheels and steered towards the door, the room was really huge.

Outside of the room the hall stretched to both sides. Gary looked left and right. *Where is the kitchen in this fortress?*

He chose the right side as it was a shorter distance. There were doors on either side of the walls. He kept pushing the wheels and his arms ached more and more.

Suddenly Gary heard a man's voice behind him say, "Where are you going?"

Gary looked back to see the man that was asleep on the couch walking towards him with a blanket wrapped around him.

Gary hesitated, then said in a low voice, "I—I was hungry."

As the man got closer, Gary saw the wrinkles on his face that were the only clue to his age, while his face looked young and resembled Jay's a little.

When the man reached Gary, he unwrapped himself from the blanket, wrapped it over Gary, and started pushing the wheelchair towards the kitchen.

The place was very big. It took them a while to get there, and the nice man kept talking about what happened.

It turned out that Gary had fainted from shock and exhaustion. He was taken to the hospital and the doctors said it was nothing bad. He just needed to eat more and get some rest after he woke up, so they discharged him, and here he was awake after two days.

"Umm…wh-who are you?" Gary asked awkwardly.

The nice man smiled and answered, "My name is Jerry, but I go by Mr. Sligmen, I'm your grandfather and you're my grandson, so you may call me whatever you like."

Gary didn't know how to ask the next question, so he left it for later.

They entered the kitchen and it was bigger than the room Gary woke up in. It had drawers and cupboards everywhere. There were two parallel tables stretched vertically across the room.

Mr. Sligmen prepared some tea for both of them and a bowl of cereal for Gary.

"We normally have breakfast in the dining room together, but all the staff is asleep now, it's still very early."

Gary didn't respond, sipping on his tea as an excuse.

"You don't need to be wary of me. I've heard what you've gone through, I'm not gonna let the same thing happen to you again," Mr. Sligmen said as he sat on the table staring out in front of him.

"I'm sorry," Gary said in a low voice.

Mr. Sligmen smiled at him. "I like you Gary, you're a really nice kid."

After breakfast, Mr. Sligmen toured Gary around the mansion-like house, and they slipped by the small library, the two dining rooms, the basement, the small living room, the study room, the gym, and the bedrooms which were closed. They finally sat down in the main living room, and Gary had picked out a book from the library that he read as he sat, while Mr. Sligmen scanned through the newspaper.

After a few hours, a young man joined them in the living room and his attention snapped towards Gary, who hadn't realized his arrival. He started heading towards Gary, saying, "Good morning, kid, you finally woke up. Thought you were gonna sleep your life away."

Gary looked up and not realizing what this young man just said, he stared and took in the young man's unique look. The young man looked like a banana, tall, blond hair, and black eyes, again just like Jay's eye. He also wore a yellow shirt and light blue jeans.

"No need to be scared, just Uncle Charlie here. You can call me Uncle Charlie!" Smiling brightly, he hoped Gary would laugh, but he just stared.

Uncle Charlie turned to Mr. Sligmen with a mock-worried face. "I heard he was tired, but this is way over the top, Dad. You sure he's okay?"

"I'm fine, I was just…this is just a lot to take in, all at once…" Gary didn't want to be rude and this man was annoying him somewhat.

At that, someone else entered the room, a young lady with long black hair and dark blue eyes with a thin long nose to center her face. A beauty had entered the room wearing a white flower print dress. Gary immediately took her for his aunt.

"Oh hello! You're Gary, aren't you! I was waiting for you to wake up! You looked exhausted. Are you alright?!" She seemed nice.

"I'm alright…" Gary said in a low voice.

"Is your voice gone? I can barely hear you!"

"Quiet down, Lucy, this kid gets scared easily, you know," Uncle Charlie said, now sitting on a couch next to his father.

"This is Lucy, Charlie's daughter," Mr. Sligmen explained, folding his newspaper. "They are an energetic and carefree pair, don't mind them."

Mr. Sligmen then put the newspaper down on the table and stood up heading towards the door.

"Um… G-Grandfather…" Gary started.

Mr. Sligmen turned to Gary and smiled again. "I won't be long, just checking on your grandmother."

"You're lucky you're a boy. A month from now all the boys go on a trip to an open field and practice shooting! It's a family tradition! I would go, but they say it's too dangerous for me because I'm a girl!" Lucy started again.

"Girls shouldn't be playing with guns, don't you think?" Gary answered, now feeling more nervous about the future.

"But I'm all grown up, I'm already 16 and not even once have I got injured during a fight! I can handle a gun!"

"You look much older than 16." As soon as he said it, Gary realized he had made a mistake while watching Lucy's expression change.

"Well, excuse me for being old!" Uncle Charlie snickered, looking at each of them.

"That wasn't—I didn't mean, I—I'm sorry, it just slipped out!" Gary stuttered.

Now that he was going to live with these new people, he didn't want to make enemies of them. Thinking about it, Gary wondered, was he an embarrassment being there?

Chapter 4
Move Forward

As time passed by, Gary got used to his new family, but his grandmother, a plump lady, tended to stay away from him. He learned that she didn't have the best relationship with his mother and that she was the person who kicked his mother out of the house. He didn't blame her.

Two days later, the doctor checked on him and he got permission to move around without the wheelchair. He got to know some of the maids that worked there, but most weren't very interactive. Although the butler was rather friendly, he didn't have much time to hang around.

It was the fourth day now, Gary walked to the dining room alone. When he entered the whole room went silent. Well, at least Uncle Charlie and his daughter did, the others weren't talking. Gary sat down and started nibbling at his pancakes when Mr. Sligmen forced a cough to draw his attention.

"Gary. There's someone coming today."

"Is it the doctor again?" Gary asked, half knowing the answer.

"No. The police station called last night. They wanted to talk to you," Mr. Sligmen answered calmly.

"Oh," Gary said, looking back at his plate, "I thought they were done with the questions. Or is it about Jay, they still don't understand why he ran away, but I don't either." Turning to Mr. Sligmen, Gary was surprised to see the look of worry on his face.

"Um...yes and no. Well, you see, someone there wants to talk to you about Jay. He's just being escorted by the police."

"Did they not find him? Is he alright?!" He looked down at his plate. Now Gary was really worried. Was his only brother de... No, he didn't want to think about it. He decided that he doesn't like his brother anymore! Why should he care?!

Looking up from his plate, he saw everyone staring at him, even his grandmother. "It can't be bad news, can it? I mean if it was, why would they want to come all the way here?!" He made up his mind. It wasn't bad news and even if it was, he wouldn't care!

The rest of the meal was silent. Gary could feel everyone looking at him, so he tried not to make eye contact and finished as quickly as he could.

The hours went by slowly. Gary had gotten another book out of the library to read, this one about mysterious and rare diseases that looked like an old used study book.

At exactly 11 o'clock, the doorbell rang and moments later one of the maids came to the living room to ask for Gary. As he got up, Gary realized the maid was Tess, a long dark-haired maid who always had her hair in two pigtails down her back. She was one of the youngest maids that worked there. She was only in-charge of cleaning the kitchen and the dining rooms. Therefore, Tess was one of the maids with the least amount of work and the most friendly of them. She was also holding a tray with a teapot and teacups.

"Are you alright? You look pale," She whispered to Gary.

"I'm fine," he answered, keeping his eyes on the ground as he walked.

Outside the door, there was a policeman Gary recognized as the one who escorted him to the funeral.

"Glad to see you're doing better," he said, waving at Gary as he approached. "They're waiting for you," he added, opening the door. Gary suddenly felt sick and, unexpectedly, very light.

Inside there were two more policemen, one next to the window opposite of the door where the other policeman stood. On the left-most couch sat an old man with graying hair and wrinkled skin. He looked a little scary with the light shining on him through the window.

Gary entered with Tess but stood next to the door as she set the tea tray on the table and left after shooting a 'don't worry' wink at Gary.

"Hello there. You must be the Gary I've heard so much about," the scary man started. When Gary didn't respond he continued. "Come sit down."

Sitting on the couch beside the old man, Gary mumbled a barely audible hello, then stared back at the old man.

"I'll introduce myself first, then. I'm Daniel, the friendly farmer from far away."

Still no reaction.

"I met your brother Jay a while back, tricky little kid. But kind of course." He had a bit of an Australian accent.

"You met Jay?!" Gary couldn't believe it! He thought they were going to bring some kind of person with tracking skills to find his brother, or hoped at least. This was more than he had hoped for. Someone knew where Jay was heading! No! He hated him! That's right, Gary hated Jay! He didn't care!

"Yes. Now, I'm going to tell you how I met your brother, but you must not interfere. I am an old man after all, and I might get mixed up." Daniel stopped, thinking by the looks of it, then continued, "Where was I? Oh yes! I'll tell you about before I met your brother. He was walking around looking for a job. He wanted money and a place to stay, but no one wanted a little kid to work for them, so he didn't succeed. Unfortunately, some thieves found him and stole the money he had. Now this is where I come in."

Gary tried not to care, but deep down, his heart was being pulled in multiple directions. Even if he chose to forget his older brother, his feelings towards him would never change, would they?!

"He was walking down the sidewalk when he collapsed. He was starved and dehydrated. He was lucky that I was doing my shopping in town that day or he would have stayed there. I carried him back to my farm. When he woke up, he was too weak to bother asking what had happened or where he was. It was easier for me this way,

I took care of him until he got back on his feet and running again. The—"

"You didn't let him stay with you?!" Gary regretted saying that out loud, it was as if he could no longer control his emotions in Daniel's presence. "So-sorry, continue."

"Mhm, yes. Then, I told him I'd let him work for me as his thank-you for taking care of him. He stayed with me for a few months. Naturally, as an old man, I watch the news, so I saw what happened to you. I called the police and told them about Jay. They came early the next day, and I took them to the room I let Jay sleep in. No one was there, he had left a note and ran away. Turns out he heard me talking to the police."

Gary was silent. He wasn't speechless, he just had too much he wanted to say.

"I brought the note he left with me," he said, taking a note out of his pocket and handing it to Gary to read.

Gary opened the note, stiffening his hand to stop it from shaking. Meanwhile, Daniel poured himself some tea.

Dear Daniel,

I'm sorry for running away, I heard you talking to the police last night. I can't go back to my family. If I did, someone important to me might be hurt because of it. I can't let that happen, they'll be better off without me. Thank you for taking care of me. I really had fun with you.

P.S. My name isn't really Gary. I thought you'd want to know that.

Daniel had finished his tea by now and was staring at Gary.

"Thank you." That was all Gary could say.

"Your brother is a very energetic and strong person when he's around others and he knows it, but that doesn't mean he's weak when he's alone. I hope they find him soon. I want to see him again, and I bet you do too."

"How would you know that?" said Gary with a sign of hurt in his voice that he didn't mean to let slip out as he looked down.

"Jay'd sometimes stare with longing into the distance when he saw a family walk by or just kids playing in the streets. It's clear he missed you. That means you were close. So you must miss him."

Gary was now fighting back tears, he didn't want to cry in front of others. Even if he was a child, he didn't feel allowed to act like one.

Daniel caught Gary's eyes shaking slightly. Without warning, Daniel got up and pulled Gary into a hug, letting Gary's head rest against his chest, so that he'll be able to cry without the concern of the others seeing.

Gary was shocked to be hugged by a stranger. This never happened before, it felt...nice. *No, I can't cry. I shouldn't cry,* he thought as he batted his eyelashes forcing his tears back. He didn't want to look weak. He wanted to put up a strong image. He wouldn't let himself cry.

Gary waited for Daniel to let him go, which took a while, then held the note towards him. Daniel looked at the note then back at Gary. "Keep it. I don't need it."

Daniel stood up and the police started making their way towards the door

"Well, I gotta go, but I'll see you again," he said while waving his hand. The next second they had left.

Gary sat in silence staring at the door. Then he heard the familiar noise of soft feet skipping across the floor. He folded the note and hid it in his pocket as Tess opened the door.

"Hey. How'd it go?" she asked.

"They still haven't found him yet, but they found someone who met him. That is why they came," he explained.

"Are you really alright with them coming right before your therapist arrives? If it were me, this would be too much," she mumbled.

"What therapist?!" Gary asked, taking note of how her face turned from worry to guilt.

"Umm…they didn't tell you? Well, you see—ju-just ask them later," she said, motioning for him to come outside as she picked up the tea tray. "I should have brought cookies too," she said to herself.

Gary and Tess walked back to the main living room together. She wasn't skipping now because she was holding the tea tray and she already knew how clumsy she was.

As Gary entered, he saw that they were all looking at him silently, so he explained as he did with Tess after he sat down.

"That wasn't nerve-wracking at all," said Lucy sarcastically as she slouched back into the sofa she sat on.

"What about the therapist?" Gary asked, looking up to see each of the adults exchanging looks.

"Where did you hear that from? You can't be serious!" Lucy said as she looked towards her father for an answer.

Mr. Sligmen then addressed Gary, saying "Look, we were planning on telling you. It just didn't seem like the right time earlier. He's only gonna be here for half an hour and you don't need to tell him anything from the first session. He's going to be coming every month from now on."

"I'm not crazy. I don't need a therapist," said Gary, looking at Lucy's shocked face.

"You're not crazy, but you are still a kid that's gone through, well, a lot. So just give it a try. If you don't need it, we'll just tell them that you don't need it," Uncle Charlie said while locking eyes with his father and nodding.

Gary got up and went for the door when Mrs. Sligmen addressed him saying, "You can ask that therapist about becoming a doctor. So if you think about it, he might not be as useless as you think."

Gary, now frozen staring at the door, looked back at his grandmother with a look of pure shock on his face.

"H-how did you know? About me wanting to become a doctor?" he asked.

"You always read those medical books so I figured as much," she stated.

"I thought you didn't like me," Gary said as he looked down at his feet.

"You're different than your mother, even if you look like her," she said in a surprisingly calm and soft voice, different from her usual rough and loud manner of speech.

Gary looked back at his grandmother for a moment then said that he needed some time alone and left for his room, deciding to take a nap before lunch.

Knock, knock, knock.

Gary turned towards the door while rubbing his eyes. It was Uncle Charlie.

"Hey, lunch is ready," he said softly before hesitantly closing the door.

Gary got up, wondering when his therapist would arrive.

After getting another silent meal, it was back to the main living room again where all was silent once more.

After a while, Tess came around again, but there was no doorbell. Did he knock?

Tess was the first one to break the silence between them.

"So did they tell you about everything now?" she asked.

"If everything is the police and the therapist, then yes."

"Oh, okay." That wasn't convincing.

"Is there more?!"

"Well, I should let them tell you. Don't worry it's not something bad or something that you need to be nervous about," she said as they arrived at the small living room.

This time Tess put the tea tray on the table and sat down on the couch opposite the young man. Gary sat next to her.

"Hi!" said the young man rather excitedly.

"Hello," responded both Tess and Gary together.

"I hope you don't mind, I asked your friend Tess to stay with us here today so you'd be more comfortable. I'm sure she'd leave if this was making you uncomfortable," he explained.

"Oh, okay. It's alright, sir."

"Just call me by my name."

Gary waited but the young man didn't add anything, so he asked, "What is your name?"

"Oh, sorry, I guess I was excited. I'm Jacob, Jacob Brett."

"Okay, Jacob," said Gary.

"So, do you wanna tell me about what happened?"

"Well, no, but I don't think I have a choice."

Jacob was taken aback at this, he was looking forward to listening to Gary's tale.

"If—if you don't wanna tell me, you don't have to. We'll just get to know each other today and you can tell me later on."

"But I don't want to talk about it," mumbled Gary.

"That's not healthy," Jacob concluded.

After a moment of silence, Tess spoke up, "Why don't you take a walk outside? The weather is nice and the flowers are in full bloom..."

"That's a great idea, nature is the best cure. Let's go," Jacob agreed as he got up and walked to the door.

Tess and Gary followed. They went outside and walked around the house, looking at the garden and talking. Jacob was mostly talking about how he knew Gary and how he wanted to meet him.

After a while they reached the main living room and Lucy spotted them through the sliding glass doors and came outside.

"Hey, what are you doing outside?!" she asked as she rushed over.

"Nature is healthy and being around it relaxes the body, so we thought we'd come outside for a bit," Jacob explained.

"Oh well, since you're already here, do you want to play a game?"

"Lucy, don't bother them," Uncle Charlie called from inside.

"No, it's okay, the session is almost over anyway. Let them play," Jacob called back, motioning for Gary to go on.

Gary followed Lucy to the swings in the middle of the garden as Jacob and Tess went inside.

"Hey, Lucy?" Gary started while swinging on the swing.

"Yeah?"

"Is there anyone else coming? I mean, other than the police and therapist?" he asked.

"No, I don't think so. Why?"

"Well, I don't know. I just thought maybe...but never mind." He pushed hard from the ground and swung up.

Lucy stared at the sky for a second, then opened her eyes wide as if she realized something.

"Gary, follow me. Quick, hurry, you slow poke!" she called back at Gary as she had already run halfway back to the living room.

Gary followed her back inside where the adults were all talking to Jacob.

"Hey, Dad, Dad, Dad!" she called as she crossed the room to stand in front of her father.

"What is it, Lucy? I was talking!" he asked, annoyed at how she ruined the good mood.

"Is Gary going to be homeschooled with me? Is he?" she asked excitedly.

"Oh, now that you mention it, is he, Dad?" he asked, turning to his father.

"Yes, I already arranged for him to start next week," Mr. Sligmen answered.

"Yes! I don't have to be all alone during the boring—" Lucy started but was cut off by Mr. Sligmen.

"Actually, Lucy, you and Gary are going to be taught separately. Since he's still young, he's gonna have a different teacher."

"What?!" Lucy said as she turned to Gary, who just shrugged in reply.

"Well, it does make sense. If Gary wants to be a doctor and you don't, then you can't study together, can you?" Mrs. Sligmen explained.

"You want to be a doctor?! You'll be just like me!" Jacob said while staring at Gary with what seemed like the excitement that Lucy just had a second ago.

"Um...yeah, I guess," Gary responded nervously.

They kept talking until it was time for Jacob to leave.

Chapter 5
Unexpected Skills

Gary's teacher was kind and patient, but he was a bit boring compared to Gary's therapist. He only talked about the things Gary had to learn and he had to teach. After a while Uncle Charlie and Mr. Sligmen got really excited about going shooting, which they had always claimed that Gary would enjoy.

The day finally came when they were to go shooting. Mr. Sligmen got in next to the driver and Uncle Charlie, Gary, and the butler sat in the back. Gary was surprised that the butler was joining them. He thought he'd stay at home with Lucy and Mrs. Sligmen.

When they got there, to the open field, they got their bags out of the trunk and told the driver to come pick them up at sunset. Gary took a walk around the place while the adults got the guns ready. There were a few signs with a red circle in the middle at one end of the field. They had some dents on them, proof that they had been used to practice shooting. At the other end of the field, there were burlap sacks stacked up on top of each other.

The adults then joined Gary behind the burlap sacks.

"Hey, Gary, check this out!" called Uncle Charlie, nodding towards the butler who had crouched down on one knee with a gun resting on one of the sacks.

The butler took aim and shot at one of the signs across the field. Gary couldn't pinpoint where the butler had hit, but by other's reactions, he figured it was a good shot.

"Old Mr. Davis has always been good with a gun," Uncle Charlie said teasingly.

"I'm just as old as you, Mr. Sligmen," the butler responded.

"Come here, Gary." Mr. Sligmen motioned from Gary's other side. He also held a gun, but this one was smaller and much shorter than the one the butler had. Mr. Sligmen showed Gary the proper way to hold the gun and how to shoot, then held the gun towards him.

"I—I can't! I don't know how to handle a gun. I'm still too young," Gary exclaimed.

"Yeah, Dad, he's still just a child," Uncle Charlie agreed. "He might look like a child, but he's more mature than any child his age. He might even be more mature than you," Mr. Sligmen said while laughing at his own joke.

"Hey, I can be mature when I need to be," Uncle Charlie claimed, failing to convince Mr. Sligmen.

After Gary tried but failed to convince Mr. Sligmen that he can't handle a gun, he was given the smallest one and reminded how to hold and aim the gun. Was he really allowed to shoot, let alone hold a gun at his age? However, something about this made him calm, maybe it was how easy the butler made it look or maybe how Mr. Sligmen believed Gary could do it.

He aimed for the middle of the red circle and concentrated on keeping his hands steady. *Bang!* Gary was pushed back by the force of the bullet and fell over, but he got up again and looked at the sign. He still couldn't tell where he'd hit.

"Wow, Gary! That shot was very good! This is your first time shooting, isn't it? Or have you been secretly training?"

"Where did I hit?" Gary asked, ignoring Uncle Charlie's joke.

"Well, you hit the sign just outside the red circle. That's pretty good," said Mr. Sligmen, looking through a pair of binoculars.

"I don't want to do that again." Gary put the gun down on the sack in front of him and stepped away.

Uncle Charlie laughed. "Don't worry, you're just young. With skills like yours, you're bound to grow to like this when you really mature," he said while looking towards Mr. Sligmen with a sneer on his face.

After a while of shooting at the targets, they moved into the woods behind the signs and started hunting. At the end of the day, they didn't catch much, only two rabbits and a few birds, most of which the butler caught. That was their dinner that day.

*

"Go call the others," said Mr. Thompson, Gary's teacher.

It had been ten years since Gary came to live with his grandparents. His teacher changed once he started studying high school level subjects. Jacob, Gary's therapist, stopped coming after the fourth session, as Gary had convinced everyone that he'd moved on and didn't need a therapist.

Gary was suspicious of his teacher. He made him take tests without telling anyone, and he was always excited about something, but he'd never tell Gary what it was. Gary still had a year left before he could go to college. He'd always talk with his teacher about the medical college he wanted to attend.

Today, not only did Mr. Thompson arrive late, he told Gary that he had a surprise and that everyone should be there to witness it unfold.

As Gary entered the living room where Uncle Charlie and his parents sat, he remembered that Lucy had work today. She was already twenty-six and had a job that allowed her to work from home most of the time.

"Aren't you going to study? Your teacher already arrived late, you should finish up as fast as you can. If you weren't homeschooled, you would have had your summer break by now," Mrs. Sligmen complained again.

"Well, he told me to come and get you. He says he has some sort of surprise and he wants all of you to be there," Gary explained.

"What are we waiting for then? I love surprises, let's see what it is," Uncle Charlie said.

"Let's go then," added Mr. Sligmen.

Entering the library, Gary saw that Mr. Thompson had put some papers on the table in front of him.

"Welcome one, welcome all," he said.

"What? Is this a show?" Uncle Charlie laughed.

"Today, you here are going to witness something Gary has accomplished without realizing he had done so," he continued, ignoring Uncle Charlie.

"Today, Gary is going to be given his reports and a very important letter."

Mr. Thompson held up the papers on the table and called out what each of them were before placing them in front of Gary and his family across the table.

"Gary's high school report cards. As you can see, they go up all the way to a twelve grader."

"Wait, what?" Mr. Sligmen asked, taken aback.

"Gary finished school a year early," Mr. Thompson explained.

"When did I do that?" Gary asked, scanning all of the report cards to see mostly *A*s and a few *B*s here and there.

"You didn't do that, I did it. Unfortunately, I was only with you for a few years, so I couldn't get you to finish any sooner, but I'm sure you would have been able to do it. As soon as I became your teacher, I realized how good you were, so I started teaching you more than it was required without telling you.

"Of course, you did great, so I thought that I might be able to get you to finish early, which I did. As you can see, you moved fast and adapted to the extra learning very well. This is where I started asking you about what colleges you had in mind," he concluded.

"I still feel like I haven't finished, like I don't know everything," Gary said, finally looking up.

"At least you're done now," Mrs. Sligmen commented.

"What about the letter, what is that?" Uncle Charlie asked, pointing at the letter on the table.

"Thank you for asking because this here is something very important. Gary, do you remember the exams I had you take?" Mr. Thompson held up the letter, hiding the words behind his hand.

"The ones you had me take in secret? Yes," Gary answered.

"Well most of them were normal exams but the last two were entrance exams. Entrance exams to get into that medical college you admire," Mr. Thompson explained.

"You got me into En Bonne Santé Medical School?!" Gary asked.

Uncle Charlie laughed, saying, "An bun san-te? Seriously?! Who came up with that name?"

"Well, this is the letter that will answer that question." Mr. Thompson held the letter towards Gary.

Gary took a deep breath and opened the letter. Spotting his name at the top made him even more nervous. He scanned through the paper and his gaze landed on one word. He read aloud: "Accepted!"

"I got accepted! I'm going to medical school!" Gary claimed, looking up at his teacher.

"Congratulations, Gary," Mr. Sligmen said, patting Gary on the shoulder.

"You could have at least told us before, now Gary's got to get ready and so suddenly!" Mrs. Sligmen sighed.

"I already taught you the basics and a little of what I think you'll take when you get there. So basically, you already got the foundation. I don't really understand it as much as you do, I don't do health and biology," Mr. Thompson explained.

Gary stared at his teacher, amazed at what he'd done and very guilty for doubting him.

"Thank you," Gary said, still staring. He meant it with every fiber of his body, if only they understood how thankful he felt at this moment. No matter how many times he said thank you and got Mr. Thompson gifts, he felt as if he could never repay his teacher. He would treasure this relationship forever.

Lucy finally joined everyone at dinner, which Mr. Thompson was invited to.

"You took a little longer than usual, did you have extra work?" Gary asked as she sat next to him on the table.

"I didn't have extra work, actually I didn't have much work to do today. My friend asked me if I could do his part too because he had some other things to do and, you know, how I just can't say no…" She sighed.

"You're too nice for your own good," Gary responded.

"Look who's talking." Lucy smirked.

"Why is everyone so worked up?" she asked, taking a bite.

"Oh, Mr. Thompson had some news. He'd taken my studies into his own hands and helped me graduate early."

"You graduated? Congrats!" She swallowed and took another bite.

"Slow down, you're going to choke!" Gary warned.

"I'm hungry."

"Do you even know what you're eating? If Grandma saw you, she'd—"

"She'd say, 'Don't eat like that! This fish is expensive, respect it!'" Lucy giggled in a hushed voice.

Gary fought back his laugh as he swallowed the fish in his mouth. Lucy had imitated Mrs. Sligmen perfectly.

The rest of the meal was mostly Uncle Charlie predicting what will happen once Gary became a doctor and teasing how serious he would be about health.

Tess entered with another maid holding dessert trays. "Do you think they'll put that time you helped me when I was sick on your record? You've got to get all the credit, I was very ill," she asked, setting the dessert down.

"I think they only count stuff that happens after I start medical school, Tess," Gary guessed.

"That's right, you also get to work in a hospital. Of course, not alone, you'll have to be with a professional doctor and one of the professors from the medical school," Mr. Thompson added.

"I'll come visit then. We'll see if you make a good doctor," Uncle Charlie teased.

"Oh, Gary, did you fill out the form I gave you?" Mr. Thompson asked.

"Yes, I did. I'll give it to you after dinner."

"Good. I have to get it back by next week. Did you choose a good major?"

"I think so, I didn't want to choose anything too easy or too hard. I'm thinking of becoming a surgeon," Gary explained.

"But won't that be hard?" Lucy asked after finishing her brownie.

"Not if I don't get too distracted. I'll have to study much more than I do now though," Gary replied.

"So you want to go around and open people to fix their bodies? Now where is the purpose of that?! Just be a normal doctor, save yourself the work," Mrs. Sligmen complained while the others laughed, knowing this would have happened sooner or later.

Chapter 6
Early Surgeon

It was Gary's third year of medical school now. He was waiting next to the front doors of the building for his professor. It was his turn to go to the hospital to watch and take note of how the doctors and surgeons diagnose the patients and reveal what surgery they have to get.

The professor was late. He seemed ill during the lecture that day, so he told Gary that they were to meet later than the appointed time. Gary was reading a book that they studied from today.

"I see you take your studies seriously, unlike some other students," Professor Gray said, appearing beside Gary.

"I'm just reviewing what we took. What about you? Are you sure you can go with me today? You seem tired." Gary closed his book.

"Oh, it's just a little cold. Besides, after today I'll have the whole weekend to rest."

"Okay."

"Come on then, we don't want to be late," Professor Gray said as he opened the door. The hospital was adjacent to the college, so they walked there.

"How long will we stay?" Gary asked.

"Until they close. They close early on weekends. We'll exit through the emergency center afterwards. The doctor assigned for today is an old friend of mine. I'd like to say hello. Oh, he also wants to meet you."

"He wants to meet me?" Gary was taken aback. *How would a doctor know about him?*

"I told him about you once, or twice. The student who always surprises everyone with his knowledge and skills. He was curious," Professor Gray explained.

"I-I'm not that good! You're overestimating me, Professor!" Gary stuttered, embarrassed by how his professor bragged about him. Professor Gray had been interested in Gary ever since he'd first taught him.

"I can tell that you're good. Just you wait, you'll change the world."

"I wouldn't say change the world…"

*

After they got there, they sat through a meeting between a doctor and a surgeon and then joined the doctor as he diagnosed some patients after a few tests and scans.

"Well, that was the last patient for today. We finished a little later than usual today, I hope you don't mind," the doctor said as he packed his stuff away and got ready to lock the room.

"It's quite alright, I was going to go say hello to Chris anyway," Professor Gray added.

"Well, don't bother him too much, he's going to be the only doctor here today. The other one is too sick to come," the doctor explained.

"It is flu season," Professor Gray added.

"Do you get a lot of patients at the emergency center?" Gary asked.

"Not usually, there's another hospital nearby, most patients go there," the doctor answered.

The doctor locked the room and said goodbye to Gary and Professor Gray, then left. Gary then followed Professor Gray to the emergency center. He was lost in thought as he stared at his professor in front of him when he realized that Professor Gray was trembling. His hands where shaking.

"Professor, are you alright? You're shaking..." Gary asked, concerned for his professor.

"I'm just a little tired, maybe a bit dizzy too. I'll be alright though, we'll just say hello and be out of there. You don't have to worry too much. I'll be able to rest soon," Professor Gray responded.

Gary didn't trust Professor Gray's words. He would have to keep an eye on him to make sure he'd be alright. Passing through the halls, Gary felt like an intruder. No one was there and the lights were off. There was a light on up ahead through the glass doors. It was the emergency center.

They passed by the reception after asking which room the doctor was using and knocked on the first door to the right. A young woman opened the door wearing a nurse's uniform. She looked confused at first.

"Can I help you, sir?" she asked.

"I'm here to see Chris, I'm an old friend of his," Professor Gray explained.

"Oh, come in. He's still not here. We called him earlier, he should be here soon." She moved aside to let them in.

There was another nurse siting behind the computer, a young man.

"I thought you were the doctor since there wasn't anything about a patient sent to the computer," The young man said.

"Professor, I don't think we should stay. You're too tired, you should get home and rest," Gary said to his professor.

"Yeah, I think... I guess we should take our leave now," Professor Gray agreed.

As they exited the room, they heard sirens from an ambulance and voices down the hall. A group of people pushing a bed with a red-haired man on it rounded the corner, heading towards them. They stopped in front of Gary and Professor Gray, and the person up-front looked into the room with the two nurses.

"Chris..." Professor Gray mumbled under his breath. He seemed to be shocked.

Gary stared at the man on the bed. He was bleeding from his right arm and had a vertical piece of metal sticking out of his body, underneath his right rib cage. He was a mess.

"Where is the doctor?" asked the guy up-front.

"That is the doctor," answered Professor Gray, staring at the man unconscious on the bed.

"What?" Both the nurses rushed out of the room to see what he was talking about.

"Who are you?" the guy up-front asked Professor Gray.

"I'm a professor from the medical school next door. I'm here with one of my students," Professor Gray responded.

"I'm the head of the emergency team. This guy's been in an accident. He needs to undergo surgery. From our evaluation, we concluded that this piece of metal has pierced his right kidney. It's bleeding too much. At this rate, he'll bleed to death. Do you think you can perform the surgery?" the guy explained.

"I—" Professor Gray started.

"You can't," Gary interrupted.

"He has to. I'm just a nurse, I only help out during surgery. I take orders, I don't give them." the young male nurse called out.

"He can't. He's sick, he's shaking, he's sweating, and his breathing is heavy. He's been working since early this morning, he's exhausted. If he performs the surgery, it'll just make things worse," Gary raised his voice now. They needed to think.

"So what do you think we should do?" Professor Gray asked Gary.

"I don't know..."

"Gary, I asked you that question because I trust you. What do you think we should do now?" Professor Gray repeated.

Gary looked around. Everyone was staring at him now. He looked down at the injured doctor, his time was depleting and fast.

"He needs a radical nephrectomy to remove the right kidney. There's no time to take tests to get him ready, and someone who knows this surgery has to do it. So I guess I can do it," Gary concluded.

"Are you crazy?" asked a women next to the bed.

"No, it's okay, he's top of his class. He's naturally skilled when it comes to medicine and health. I'm sure he can pull this off," Professor Gray explained.

"Can't you just call another doctor or another professor?" asked the same woman.

"The professors have all gone home by now," Professor Gray said.

The female nurse rushed back into the room and reached for the phone. After a minute or so, she returned.

"The only doctor I could get a hold of is going to take at least an hour to get here," she reported.

"It's decided then, Gary's going to perform the surgery. Even if I want to do it, I can't, I only do tests and scans," Professor Gray said.

"You two get him ready, put him under anesthetics. I'll take it from there," Gary told the two nurses with as much confidence as he could. He didn't feel confident at all. He felt nauseous and frightened, but he followed behind them nonetheless.

Professor Gray followed beside him as well. Gary realized he was right to stop him from performing the surgery. His hands were shaking badly, his steps were uneven, and he wasn't walking in a straight line.

"Professor, go rest. If you keep pushing yourself, we'll have two people to take care of. Besides, you're barely standing," Gary told his professor.

"I know, I will. It's just, you don't have a license so you're not supposed to be doing this, I have to be there to supervise you."

"It's alright. I know what I'm doing. Trust me and go get some rest. When you open your eyes, the surgery will be over," Gary tried to persuade Professor Gray.

Professor Gray looked at his friend being pushed into the surgery room, then back at Gary. He sighed.

"Fine, I trust you," he said as he headed back to reception.

Gary was ready to go in now. He looked down at his hands, they were shaking and he was nervous. He closed his eyes, took a deep breath, paused before breathing again, and opened his eyes. His nerves were a little bit better and his hands had steadied. He pushed the doors and entered.

The two nurses had already put on their surgical aprons. "Is everything ready?" Gary asked.

"Yes, we're just waiting to start," the male nurse answered.

For the doctor's right arm, Gary disinfected the wound and stitched it up. The kidney was next.

"First, we'll have to remove the metal piece. It's shaped like a sword but uneven on the edges. I'm guessing there's intensive internal bleeding. So pulling it out first isn't an option.

"We'll have to get the kidney ready for removal before pulling it out. That will make sure he doesn't lose any more blood. But he'll still need blood transfusion. Do any of you know his blood type?" Gary analyzed.

"I do, I'm new so I had to read both of their files," the female nurse responded, looking at the other nurse.

"Then go and get the blood ready for transfusion," Gary ordered.

Gary looked down at the piece of metal. It looked to be about eight inches long and less than an inch wide, almost perfect.

Gary cut beneath the metal in a vertical line, following the injury down. Only four inches. Now he needed to cut the ureter away from the kidney. It was a little hard seeing it from underneath the metal piece.

"Can one of you get some gauze and hold the incision open so I can see?" Gary asked.

The male nurse did as he said.

"Don't pull too hard, the injury didn't make a clean cut." Gary warned.

Carefully, Gary cut away the ureter. He stared cutting the blood vessels away from the kidney. He couldn't reach all of them. He tied them up so it wouldn't cause more bleeding. Gary then cut away all the connected muscles, fat, and tissues that he could see, but he needed to remove the metal piece to get to the rest.

Now he carefully pulled the metal piece out of the body. As soon as he did, the kidneys' bleeding intensified. It was a good thing that they prepared it for removal. Now all was left was cutting away the remaining blood vessels, muscles, fat, and tissues.

"Could you take that metal tool and hold the ribs up?" he asked the female nurse, pointing at a bent metal tool on one of the trays.

As she pulled the ribs back, Gary felt relieved. This type of surgery made it possible that he might have to remove one of the ribs, but it looked like that wouldn't be a problem, so he didn't have to remove it.

He quickly cut away the remaining blood vessels and tied them up to the others. He cut the remaining muscles, fat, and tissues, then carefully removed the kidney. It had already stopped bleeding, which made it easier to see.

They cleaned up the blood and checked that the blood transfusion was going smoothly, then Gary started to cut away the injured tissues and disinfecting the wound. The incision was closed with a few stitches and they were done. "One of you should stay with him until he wakes up just in case," Gary advised.

"Thank you. You really helped us," the female nurse said.

"No, I wouldn't trust myself. A doctor should double-check everything to make sure I didn't do anything wrong. I should be thanking you for helping me. I didn't ask for your names, did I?" Gary added.

"I'm Alicia," the female nurse responded.

"I'm Max," the male nurse added.

"I'm Gary."

Gary went to look for his professor, but he didn't find him anywhere. There were a few patients, so he went to see the doctor. He knocked on the door and entered just as a mother with a baby in her hands was about to leave. Behind the desk, there was a man with graying hair and glasses.

"Hello, I'm Gary, a student from next door. Have you seen a professor around?" Gary asked him.

"So you're the one who did the nephrectomy. I met your professor and told him to go home, he looked tired. You took a long time, almost five hours. You should call him though, he didn't look very calm," the doctor said, without a change in expression.

Chapter 7
News

A week had passed since the night Gary performed the surgery. He came back home exhausted and got told off by his grandmother. It was clear she was worried, but she still acted as if she were angry. He went to bed that night after telling everyone that it was an emergency and not really explaining what happened. He also called Professor Gray using the house phone and told him that everything was fine now.

It was Friday again. Gary went home straight after he finished classes this time. He excused himself to his bedroom to study. His end of term exams were near, he had to be prepared.

After a while, Tess came knocking at his door saying there were visitors that came for him. She said to go to the main living room, but that wasn't where they usually had guests. *Who could it be?* he thought.

It was Professor Gray, the doctor named Chris, and Alicia and Max, the nurses. They were all sitting down on the long couch that Mr. and Mrs. Sligmen usually sat on.

This time Mr. and Mrs. Sligmen were sitting on the smaller couch closer to the door.

"Why are you here? Are you okay?" Gary asked Chris.

"I'm fine thanks to you. I wouldn't have believed it was you who did the surgery if William here wasn't the one who told me," he responded, pointing his thumb at Professor Gray beside him.

"You didn't tell us you performed a surgery on a doctor," Lucy said. She sat beside her father.

"I was tired and you didn't ask," Gary explained. "Is that why you're here? Am I going to have to sign some files or something?" Gary said, sitting down.

"No, we came to thank you, and when word spread about what you did, I was able to do something for you," Professor Gray said.

"What did you do?" Gary asked.

"You know about the practical exam, right?" Professor Gray asked.

"We have a practical exam? I thought we only had one at the end of the year..." Gary responded.

"No, you're right. I didn't say you'd have one now, I mean the one at the end of the year. I should have explained, you have exams coming up, I forgot."

"It's alright. What about the practical?" Gary asked. "Well after some scans and some checks with other doctors, we concluded that you had done a good job with Chris."

"It was, you can say, a perfect surgery," Chris added. "So I was able to get the one who was grading the practical exam to take your performance in this surgery into account. But he said at first that the surgery you performed was harder than the exam that you were going to take. So he gave you extra marks," Professor Gray explained.

"Wait, but I didn't even do anything," Gary gasped.

"What do you mean you didn't do anything? You cut that old man open and fixed him!" Mrs. Sligmen spoke up.

"I'm not that old..." Chris added in a low voice.

"Wait, so what do I do when the exam comes up? Will it be different for me?" Gary asked.

"You don't have to take it anymore, you've already passed and with more than a hundred percent," Professor Gray assured Gary.

"Is getting more than a hundred percent even possible?" Uncle Charlie asked.

"Well the extra marks will go to the rest of his studies, other than the practical," Professor Gray explained.

"You might just be the best doctor of the century," Chris added.

"No, I still need to study more. There was a tool I didn't know the name of, and if it was something other than a nephrectomy, I don't think I'd have been able to do it. You're lucky I studied this," Gary explained to Chris.

"They teach you these things at that medical school? Aren't you too young to be studying about things this detailed?" Chris asked.

"No, I studied this by myself, I like to study about these things," Gary explained.

"You should have seen him when he was younger. He always had his face in a book, reading about famous doctors and rare diseases," Mr. Sligmen added teasingly.

"It was scary really. He'd come tell us about these rare diseases and their symptoms. I was scared I might have one," Mrs. Sligmen complained while they all laughed.

They talked through the afternoon and soon Professor Gray, Chris, Alicia, and Max took their leave.

A few weeks later as the weather got colder, there came news of Lucy's mother's death. She had died in a car accident while traveling. Her job required a lot of traveling, which was why she wasn't around much. Gary walked through the garden towards Lucy, who was swinging on the swings alone. He remembered when they were younger and had Fred come over. Lucy never had a friend her age before and even though she was more than five years older than Fred and Gary, she still had a lot of fun.

"Hey," Gary said awkwardly as he sat on the swing next to Lucy.

"Hey," she responded.

"Are you alright?" he asked, swinging gently.

"I'm fine, really, I didn't know her that much so it's not like I'm going to become a crazy depressed person. I just need some time to think," she answered in what seemed to be an annoyed voice, but Gary understood. He didn't want to push her.

"It's okay if you don't want to talk about it. I'll just keep you company as you think it through," Gary concluded.

Lucy turned to look at him as if to respond but looked away and kept swinging gently. Gary knew what she was thinking: she didn't want him to keep her company, she wanted to be alone. He wanted to respect that and leave her to her thoughts, but he knew how it felt to lose someone.

Even if he didn't like his mother, she was still his mother. He ended up pushing away all the help he got, convincing himself that he hated his mother and didn't need help coping with his emotions. That resulted in him growing up with many insecurities, and even if he seemed confident on the outside, he would always doubt himself secretly. He didn't want that to happen to the fun and energetic Lucy.

He remembered when he asked about her mother when they were kids. She had explained why her mother wasn't around and told him how her father and mother were divorced. He felt guilty for asking, but she assured him that it wasn't because they hated each other, but they just didn't agree and wanted different things so they thought it would be best to split up and remain as friends. She visited from time to time to check up on Lucy and the rest of them.

"Gary?" she asked, still looking at the ground in front of her.

"Yeah?"

"Did you like your mother? I mean, I know that she wasn't that nice to you and all, but did you miss her after she died?"

Gary stared at Lucy for a second, surprised that she asked this question. He wanted to say yes and ask if he's crazy for feeling this way, even though she was nothing more than a bully to him. But he didn't want to confuse Lucy and turn the attention to himself. She needed the attention more than him now. She needed to open up to feel better.

"No," he said.

"I thought you might say that. I don't miss her much either and I feel guilty for it. She got me gifts every time she came to visit. She loved me, but I barely knew her." She seemed like she wanted to say more but stayed quiet.

"Lucy, if you were in a bad situation, who would you think of?" Gary asked.

"You guys. You, Dad, Grandma, Grandpa and maybe Tess and Fred. They used to play with us when we were younger and we still have fun when we're together," she said without emotion.

"So, if you were to…uhh, if you were to leave and never come back, what would you want to happen to us?"

"You mean if I died."

"Well, it doesn't have to—"

"I'd want you all to stay the way you were before and live happy lives. I wouldn't be able to come back to life, so why should you be suffering," she answered.

"Well, your mother must have thought of you before it happened. She must have wanted you to be happy."

"But I can't just be happy when everyone else and Dad, most of all, are upset."

"You don't have to be happy right away. You can be sad at first. Besides, with every action, there is an equal and opposite reaction. So if you're sad now, you're bound to be happy later on, or the other way around. It's just how life works. So you can feel any way you want now, but don't let it take over your life."

"Did you just use Newton's law with emotions?!" asked Lucy, giggling slightly.

"Maybe." Gary smiled.

"Don't worry, I have more control over my emotions than you'd think," she reassured Gary.

Chapter 8
Graduation Project

Gary had his twenty-fourth birthday a while ago and was about to graduate medical school. Everyone graduating was supposed to submit a graduation project within two months, where they'd demonstrate their skills.

Some of the people in Gary's class worked with doctors in the hospital and others worked with professors. Gary worked alone. He also got permission to use one of the labs after sunset.

Gary worked on a cat he found while on his way back home. He wasn't studying animals or thinking of working at a vet, but this cat seemed tired and he wanted to help it. After asking his professor if he could work on the cat as his graduation project, he started running tests and reading up on cats. He thought it would be easy to help this cat, but no matter how many tests he ran on her, he couldn't figure out what she had.

It was almost twelve at night. Gary was looking at the information he had gathered up so far, trying to pinpoint what was wrong. He was staring at the computer with his back to the lab.

"The bloodstream seems to be the most infected area. But how did it get infected? It must have come from the heart since it's the organ that has the most influence on the blood. I already gave her some medicine for that, but every time her heart is 'infection free,' it just gets infected again after a while. Then it must be somewhere else. The infection must be hiding somewhere that can trick a person into thinking it's in the heart from the bloodstream. It can't be the lungs, since it's only infected where it connects with the arteries and veins. The kidney filters the blood so it wouldn't—" Gary was muttering to himself when he was cut off.

"Why does it have to be connected to the bloodstream?" Lucy asked, making Gary jump and hit his elbow on the edge of the table, sending a sensation of lightning passing through the bones in his arm. Lucy giggled at what she had caused.

"Are you okay?" she asked, still giggling.

"You scared me! I could have had a heart attack! I could have hit you!" Gary stressed, annoyed at how funny Lucy thought all of this was.

"Anyway. Grandma says you should get back soon. It's getting annoying how she keeps fussing about you staying here so late. So I came to get you. I did knock before coming in, you know," Lucy explained after calming down.

She walked over to the cat sleeping on the other side of the table and petted her gently as not to wake her up.

"Is Cookie still not getting any better?" she asked.

"No, but I gave her some medicine for her fever, so she isn't doing that bad. Before today, I was so focused on the heart that I forgot about the other organs that can influence the bloodstream. So I'm trying to find out where the infection could be hiding so I can cure her," Gary explained, putting his files away and getting ready to leave.

"Can't you just scan her?" Lucy asked, putting the cat carefully into the carrier she bought for her.

"I did. The infection is all over her body, but it's mostly concentrated in her heart so I thought that's where it was hiding in, like a base. Turns out I was wrong."

"You have to cure her, Gary. You can't let Cookie die. Why don't you just take her to the vet?"

"I did. The medicine they gave me isn't working. They were the ones who told me it was in the heart."

"Then it has to be somewhere else? Like the lungs and kidney? But aren't the lungs concentrated on the air more than the blood?" Lucy asked.

"Well, the lungs exchange the carbon dioxide in the blood with oxygen. So if the infection was hiding there, it would have entered the bloodstream with the oxygen," Gary explained, closing the door after Lucy joined him in the hall. There was a light up the hall, but they were going the other way.

"And the kidney?"

"Well, the kidney filters the blood, but it also returns some of the electrolytes. So the infection could mix in with it and—" Gary stopped in his tracks.

"Lucy, you said before that Cookie didn't urinate much, didn't you?" Gary asked, taking the carrier from Lucy's hands.

"You're finally using her name! But yeah, I bought her a litter box, but she didn't use it much and when she did, it always left a gross smell," Lucy explained.

"Okay, thanks." Gary said turning around.

"Tell Grandma that I'll be late," he added, walking as fast as he could while holding the carrier with both hands. He was heading for the light. Professor Gray was going to be working late today. Maybe he could get him to scan her kidneys to get a clearer picture on the nephrons.

Gary had a hunch that the infection was entering the bloodstream through the reabsorption of electrolytes from the nephrons in the kidneys. If that was true, it would explain the extra electrolytes in the blood that always showed up in his tests. It could be that the blood was reabsorbing too much electrolytes.

Professor Gray was about to leave when Gary approached him. He asked if he could scan Cookie and Professor Gray told Gary to scan her himself and gave him the keys. He was right, but it was too late do anything about it that night, so he went home and told his grandmother, who was waiting for him, that he wouldn't be late again and this time he wasn't lying because he finally figured it out.

After sunset the next day, Gary went back to the lab and started working on the new medicine. It took a few hours to finish. It was a serum that had to be injected, so Gary got a needle and filled it up. As soon as he injected the serum into Cookie, her muscles relaxed. He was excited. He felt like he finally achieved something after all his failed attempts, but he had to wait a couple of days to be sure.

After a week, give or take, Cookie was much healthier and more energetic than before. Gary wrapped up his report and gave it to the professor in charge the next day.

"Thank you, Gary. I thought you'd be late, but it looks like you finished in half the time. How is the cat doing now?" the professor asked.

"She's alright. My family thought that it'd be nice to keep her, so now she's kind of our pet," Gary explained.

"Well it's nice that she ended up...well. It really surprised me to find out that you were having trouble, so I was looking forward to reading your report. I guess I'll just have you tell me about it later," sighed the professor, holding the papers back towards Gary, who started to panic. Why wouldn't they accept his project?

"W-What do you mean. I don't understand. I even got permission to work on Cookie, I-I mean the cat," Gary stuttered, taking the papers back. He felt more nervous and anxious by the second.

"You have been selected to take part in a special, early graduation exam with a few other students. Everyone who was selected doesn't need to work on a graduation project or hand in any of the homework assignments," the Professor explained, smiling.

"I still don't think I fully understand, Professor," Gary said, still very nervous.

"I'm not sure of the details, but I do know this—you will have to go to a meeting with all the students that have been chosen and the people who chose you. You start next week. I didn't tell you because I wanted to see if you could figure out what was going on with that cat."

"The people who chose us?"

"They are from the government. I think they want to be ready, just in case this disagreement with the country next door turns into a war. You know, have good doctors ready." The professor said, looking at Gary's confused look.

"War? What war?"

"You really are late on the news, aren't you? A few weeks ago, our president had a disagreement with the president from the country next door and rumor has it, a war is about to start," explained the professor.

"So they want me as a doctor in the war?" Gary asked.

"I think so. You see, there was an outbreak of a virus in the capital and it's spreading. So they can't send any of the experienced doctors; they need them to take care of things."

"A virus and a war?!" Gary asked himself. He didn't know if he believed it or not.

"You should watch the news now and then. People would think you live under a rock."

The professor gave Gary an envelope which he said would tell him what was going to happen now since he was chosen. After that Gary went back home. He went to his room and dropped his stuff, then went to the main living room where everyone was gathered.

"You're back early," said Uncle Charlie.

"Yeah, I was uh...I was chosen for this thing, so I don't really have to attend any classes until next week," Gary explained.

"So you got suspended? Just when I thought we'd had a normal person in this house," Mrs. Sligmen complained.

"I'm normal!" shot Mr. Sligmen at his wife. Uncle Charlie and Lucy, who had Cookie on her lap, didn't even try to protest. They knew that Mrs. Sligmen always thought they were the weird bunch of the family.

"I'm not suspended. But, um, do any of you know about the virus in the capital?" Gary asked.

"Oh, I've heard of it from my co-workers. They said it was very dangerous and the whole capital is on lockdown." Lucy said, scratching behind Cookies ears.

"It's lucky we live far from the capital," Uncle Charlie added.

"But I'm sure the doctors will find a cure soon," Mr. Sligmen said turning to Gary.

"So, then, what about the war?" Gary continued.

"See, I told you it was a war, they're going to kill us all." Mrs. Sligmen complained, looking at Mr. Sligmen.

"We can't just jump to conclusions. It's just a little fight that they had, they're only humans," Mr. Sligmen said.

"I'm not too sure about that," Gary said.

"See!" Mrs. Sligmen, still looking at Mr. Sligmen, pointed at Gary.

"What do you mean?" Lucy asked.

"Well, my professor told me that the thing that I was chosen for had something to do with the government. Also, since the doctors are busy trying to figure out this thing with the virus, they can't be of any help if the war really does start so, they need more doctors," Gary explained, motioning to himself.

Everyone started talking all at once, but Gary put his hand up to silence them. Everyone stopped talking except Mrs. Sligmen, who stood up now.

"...you to go to war so, the country would be safe? Do they really think that sending some medical students would help the chances of us winning this war? You will not go! I won't allow it! They can't take you!" she shouted.

Gary got up and started towards her when she passed him, heading for the door. She slammed the door on her way out.

Gary stood there, staring at the door, and everyone was silent for a moment, then Mr. Sligmen got up and went after her.

"You're really going to be sent to the war?" Lucy asked.

"I'm not sure. They'll tell us next week." Gary sat back down. The room suddenly felt much smaller. The sunlight from the glass doors seemed very bright. The air in the room felt heavy and still.

Cookie jumped down from Lucy's lap and walked lazily to Gary, jumped up and laid down on his lap.

"Try not to talk about it when your grandma is around," Uncle Charlie warned.

"I know. I shouldn't have said anything until I was sure," Gary blamed himself, now gently petting Cookie.

After a while, Gary felt uncomfortable sitting there. He excused himself and went back to his room. He opened his report and read it again. He worked so hard for nothing.

At least, Cookie was better. He opened the envelope and read through it. They'd meet at eight in the morning on Monday and a government official would explain everything.

They had to bring the first-aid bag they were given on their first day of medical school. It was a small white sling backpack that had pockets on the inside which were shaped to carry different types of tools and medicine. There were many tools in the pockets, none of them used. There were some alcohol sterilizing wipes in one of the zipped-up pockets.

Gary walked to his desk and picked up the small bottles next to his report. The antidote he brewed for Cookie had some left over, which he bottled up in these small glass bottles. He hid all three of them in the pocket filled with alcohol wipes and zipped it closed. After putting the envelope and a pen in the bag and setting it aside, Gary flopped down on his bed and stared up at the ceiling.

How could the professor talk about a war so calmly? Was he relieved that he wasn't the one selected to go to the war? Gary couldn't bring himself to blame him, he would have felt the same way. It was his fault for standing out. Did Jay know about the war? What about the virus? Was he in the capital? Was he alright now? Did he have enough money to take care of himself now? Wait...what was Gary thinking? He should just forget about Jay already and move on. Jay didn't care about him so why should Gary care about Jay? Because he still missed him? Because it still hurt when he remembered everything that had happened? Because it was all his fault?

The rest of the week passed by very slowly and no one mentioned anything about the war, the virus, or the capital. Gary spent most of the week in his bedroom studying for the exams that he'd take the next week, which were mentioned on the papers in the envelope. He tried to study.

He didn't feel very motivated to pass these exams since he'd most likely be sent to war if he did. He would lay his head on his desk, using the open book as a pillow and think about anything else. Sometimes he found himself imagining that Jay came knocking on the door after hearing about Gary being sent to war. He would stop himself halfway, reminding himself that the police never found him. He was already dead, he didn't matter.

When Gary sat with the others in the main living room, he sometimes caught them exchanging looks. Mrs. Sligmen didn't talk at all after that day. She kept reading the newspapers, even the old ones. The day came when Gary had to go to the meeting and confirm what would happen next.

Chapter 9
War

He looked at himself through the mirror. He looked very professional, like a real doctor. He had this uniform in his closet from the first day of medical school. They gave it to him along with the first-aid bag, but wearing it wasn't mandatory. He wore a white button-up shirt with the countrywide health logo of a bird's wing with a heartbeat on it on the left chest, which was tucked in his white trousers. He grabbed the knee-length white coat off of his bed and put it on before swinging the small first-aid sling backpack over his shoulder and heading for the door. Gary met Tess in the hallway, who told him that breakfast was ready. That was weird. Gary always had breakfast at the cafeteria. Why had they made breakfast for him? His question was answered when he stepped into the dining room. Mrs. Sligmen was sitting in her usual place at the head of the table, with a plate of sausages and an egg sunny side up, untouched. "Today's paper came," she said.

"Grandma, why are you up so early? I can tell you everything when I come back. You shouldn't worry so much."

"It's confirmed. We're officially at war." She raised her voice now. Her words were like a stab to the heart. Gary had been hoping that it would be anything else.

Gary realized he was staring emotionlessly at Mrs. Sligmen. He sat down and stuffed his face before he could lose control of his emotions. He felt his eyes heat up as he fought back the tears. He felt an invisible rock clogged in this throat, but he forced himself to swallow even if it felt like the rock got bigger with each passing second. His stomach didn't want to accept the food; he didn't know if it would all come back up or not.

"Gary, you have to fail their exams," Mrs. Sligmen pleaded, snapping Gary out of his silent mental breakdown.

Gary swallowed and put his fork down. "I can't do that. You know they wouldn't believe me if I did," Gary said in an attempt to calm himself.

It was silent for a while again until Mrs. Sligmen got up and sat next to Gary, where Lucy always sat.

"Gary, you know how I can't stop myself from worrying about everyone and I may not have the best way of showing it, but you can't go to war. It's too dangerous. What if you died? What am I supposed to do then? I never apologized for treating you as if you were your mother when you were young. I didn't even wait to see the person you were. I just decided you had to be just like her and hated you.

"But I was wrong! You're not like her. You are so much more than she could have ever been. I regret every moment I disrespected you in the past! I'm so sorry. I wish

I could take it back. But if you go to war, I would never be able to make it up to you. I love you, I can't let you die hating me, and yes, I may be selfish when I say this, but I want you to love me as much as I love you. B-but, if you die—" She started crying so hard she couldn't finish her sentence.

Gary smiled and hugged her. She held him tight as if it were the last time she'd ever hold him. "Grandma, I do love you, very much. I don't care about what happened in the past as long as you've accepted me. So I won't die out there. Even if I'm in a situation where my safety isn't guaranteed, I'll live through it and come back because I love you," Gary said, convincing himself that he'd live. He felt guilty of comforting himself when Mrs. Sligmen was the one crying, but he felt no tears in his eyes. They weren't dry, but there was no trace of the tears that were just there.

"You already said that." She laughed through her tears.

"I know. That's because I really do love you. You're not just my grandma, you're my mom. And I love you for that," he stressed. Gary pulled back from Mrs. Sligmen's arms and looked her in the eyes. "That's also why I want you to let me go. I don't want to be scared for the rest of my life. So let me face my fears so that I don't feel trapped. Please!" Gary kept his eyes locked in a fixed position, staring at Mrs. Sligmen.

She looked away. "I knew you'd say that. You're a doctor, of course you'd want to save lives. That's why I told the butler to go and train with you. You'll need to learn how to protect yourself," she said.

He's a doctor, of course he'd want to save lives. Was that why he wanted to go? Did he even think of the fact that he'd save people if he went? He just thought that he'd die if he went. He was scared of that, but he didn't want to fear death. Was that selfish of him?

"You really look like a real doctor in that get-up," Mrs. Sligmen said, cutting off Gary's train of thought.

"It says that I have to wear this. I've seen many people wear it. I didn't think it'd look good on me," Gary explained.

"You definitely look very handsome," Mrs. Sligmen complimented.

Gary sat down on one of the chairs in the room. It was one of the largest rooms in the building, yet there were no more than thirty people there, all wearing the same uniform with their own first-aid sling bags. There was still a little bit of time until the meeting was to begin, but Gary couldn't see anyone other than students in the room. They were all sitting on a chair. The chairs were arranged in one big semicircle in the middle of the room. After a while a group of people entered through the door, some wearing suits and the rest wearing military uniforms. They headed towards the long table and sat behind it, facing the students. They were very organized. They were all ready to start.

"Some of you might know that there will be a war soon. Our country is at a disadvantage with this virus going around. So the doctors we already have aren't able to help us in this war. We need qualified doctors, people who know what they're doing. We have gathered the most outstanding medical students in the country. You will be tested and trained, we need you to help us defend our country," said one of the men wearing a suit and sitting in the middle. The students just stared.

"Let me handle the talking," said the man next to him wearing a military uniform. Gary didn't know much about the military, but he could tell that that man was highly ranked by the difference of his uniform from the rest of the military men's uniforms. He stood up with his hands behind his back. "You have come here to study health, right?! You want to become doctors, right?! So do your job! There's no time for lazing around! So get up!" His words echoed around the room and all of the students got up. Some of them, including Gary, hesitated, wondering if he said it as a figure of speech or as a command.

"From this day onward, you will be tested on your knowledge! You will be trained with guns! You will train your body and prepare to become real doctors! You will help us save this country! You will do this because this is the chance you were given to prove yourself! Will you fulfill your duty to this country?!" he shouted.

"Y-yes, sir," some of the students replied with weak voices.

"I don't think this will be of any help. Will you do your job?!" the man asked again.

"Yes, sir!" replied Gary and the rest of the students. Was it just him or was that man scary?

The man wearing the military uniform explained what they were going to do in more detail. After they were done, he said he would have them do a little exercise as punishment for being so shy. Ten laps around the building, ten squats, ten pushups, ten sit-ups and after seeing how tired everyone was, he said he'd let them do something less tiring. All thirty of the students were given guns and told to shoot at the tree stumps behind the building to make sure no one was in the way or got injured. After a few shots, Gary felt a pat on his shoulder. He turned to see the same high-ranked military man beside him.

"You've got talent. You've done this before?" he asked, staring at the spot on the stump where all the bullets hit. Gary didn't respond. He didn't even realize that he'd gone silent and just stared at the man.

"Come with me for a bit," he said, pulling Gary away. The student standing behind Gary stepped forward and started to shoot.

"You've got a steady hand, a sharp eye, and skill, lots of skill. You're even better than some of my men," he continued.

"It's a tradition in my family. We'd go hunting sometimes, so I got used to it," Gary explained, walking beside the man.

The man stopped and stared at Gary, who stopped and looked back.

"Tristan!" the man yelled.

Another younger man wearing a military uniform and holding a plastic water bottle ran up to them.

When he arrived next to them, the man finally took his eyes off of Gary and turned to Tristan.

"Get me a, um, never mind." He took the water bottle out of Tristan's hand and the gun from Gary's. He tossed the gun in the air and caught it again.

"I'm going to stand in front of that tree, with this bottle on my head. I want you to shoot the bottle," he explained, pointing at the farthest tree from them and the closest one to the wall that surrounded the school.

"What?!" Tristan gasped. The man held the gun out towards Gary.

"S-sir, I can't," Gary stuttered. What if he shot him?

"Okay then, I'll have the bottle on my head and you'll have to shoot while I do the squats. Anything else to say?" he asked as if it were a warning.

Gary knew that if he said anything else, it'll only get worse. "No, sir," he responded reluctantly.

"You got to work on your voice. Stop it from sounding so weak," the man said as he walked away towards the tree.

"I'll never get him," Tristan sighed.

As the man arrived at the tree, he put the bottle on his head and started doing the squats. He was surprisingly very good at balancing the bottle on his head while doing the squats.

Gary took a deep breath and raised the gun. Something about the gun looked weird. It was the safety switch. It was switched to 'safe.' Gary switched it back to 'fire.' When he looked back up, he saw the man smiling. Did he do it on purpose?

Gary aimed the gun once more. There was a split second where the man stopped moving between squats.

Gary aimed the gun at the highest point the bottle could reach as to only hit the bottle. He steadied his hands and focused. He blocked out all the sounds around him. Everything slowed down in his eyes. The man was moving very slow, slow enough for Gary to hit the bottle on time. He waited for the man to reach the peak of his squat and pulled the trigger.

The bang from the shot echoed around in the silence. As Gary watched, the bottle flew off of the man's head and slammed into the tree behind, before falling to the ground. The man stood up and turned around. He bent down and picked the bottle up. It had a hole right at the top below the neck, there was only little water remaining in the bottle. Gary gave a sigh of relief, when he heard some clapping. He turned and saw the students and men staring at them. Some were nodding, some were smiling and looking at each other, while others were clapping.

"Wow, you're good. I think I've just taken a liking to you," Tristan said, looking at Gary.

Gary, embarrassed by all the attention, looked back at the man who had walked over to him by now.

"Please don't ask me to do anything like that again," Gary said, holding the gun back towards the man.

The man took it as he laughed at Gary's words. "You have a talent in something you don't like. Strange. You are definitely a strange man," he replied.

As soon as Gary got back home, he was surrounded. Everyone was worried because he was late. He explained the exercise they had to do and told them how tired he felt, so they let him sit down first.

"So what did they say?" Mr. Sligmen asked.

"They are going to test us to see how much we know. Then, we'll be trained and sent to the camps," Gary explained.

"Camps?" Lucy asked.

"They're already setting up their base. They don't want to let the fight spread all over the country, so they'll try to keep the fight as close to the borders as possible."

"So you are being sent to war," Uncle Charlie pointed out.

"Yes, but just as a doctor, so I'll be safe. The only time a doctor goes to the battlefield is after a fight is over to look for any survivors and help them. So you don't have to worry about me."

"That doesn't change the fact that you will be going," Uncle Charlie said.

"But the chances of something happening to me are very slim. The percentage of death in war due to injury is a single digit."

"Don't lie, Gary," Mr. Sligmen said, amazed at Gary's obvious lie.

"I'm not lying. The most it could be is a five percent chance for anyone like me," Gary replied.

"Really?" Lucy asked.

"Yes. I'm telling the truth. You don't have to worry."

"Okay then, we won't fuss about it," Mrs. Sligmen concluded. Everyone went silent and turned to Mrs. Sligmen. Did she just do the opposite of complaining?

"Thank you, Grandma," Gary broke the silence.

"Wait, you're not the least bit concerned that Grandma just agreed to this?" Lucy asked, turning to Gary.

"Well, I said I didn't want anybody to make a fuss about this, so I'm happy she's willing to drop this conversation," he said. Everyone stared at him for a while.

"But yes, I think she may be a little dizzy. Are you feeling alright?" Gary asked.

"I'm doing fine! You have exams, so go study! We don't need another drop-out!" she complained.

"I'm not a drop-out, the teachers didn't know how to teach, that's all!" Uncle Charlie said.

Gary grinned as he left the room to go study.

Chapter 10
Training

The week passed by faster than Gary had expected. It was the last day of exams, while the rest of the school still had a week before exams started. Today Gary had three exams, yet he barely studied for them. He couldn't find any energy to care about these exams, but he didn't find the exams to be that hard. After they finished with the last exam, they were told to go back to the meeting room. This time there were only men wearing suits there. The military men were only present the first day.

"So finally done with exams huh? But don't celebrate yet. Your marks come out next week and only those who pass will continue with us," said a man in a suit.

A student sitting beside Gary raised his hand, and the man nodded towards him.

"What happens if we fail?" he asked.

"I doubt you will, but if that does come to pass, then you will get to retake the exams with the rest of your peers," the man in the suit answered. He explained where they would meet up, the time, and what they would be doing exactly. The meeting ended and everyone went home. If Gary passed, this would be his last weekend with his family. This was the last time he would see his family before the war.

They had a big fancy dinner that night to celebrate the end of the exams. Everyone praised Gary, but he could tell that they weren't being completely honest with him. He was sure that they didn't agree with him leaving, but it wasn't in their hands, he had no choice.

It was very early, the sun wasn't up yet, and it was still dark out. Gary was zipping up his duffle bag. He was almost ready to leave for the training center that had been set up for them. A bus was going to go to all the students to pick them up one by one, then take them to their dormitories.

Gary checked the first-aid bag one last time. All his tools were in their places, the medicine would be provided at the camps, so they didn't need to take any with them. Gary didn't bother checking on the tools. He zipped up the sling bag and picked up his duffle bag. He looked at his room one last time.

It looked so big when he first woke up here, but now it felt small and comfortable. He would miss this place. The papers on his desk caught his eye, it was the project he never had to do. This started everything that was happing. If they had just accepted his project and let him continue with the rest of the graduates, he wouldn't have had to worry about war and death. Someone knocked on the door. It was Lucy.

"Gary, come have breakfast with us. Tess made it herself," she said. The dress she was wearing was similar to the dress she had on when Gary first met her, except for the colors. Her old dress had very bright colors, but this one only had dark shades of yellow and orange.

"You didn't have to wake up so early," he replied, walking towards her.

"Well, we all wanted to say goodbye before you leave. Tess also wanted to cook you something special. You know she doesn't cook, so this means that she was practicing. She really feels in debt to you," Lucy explained.

"She works here! We are the ones in debt to her," Gary fussed.

"Hey, try to understand how she feels," Lucy lectured.

"I know, I know. It's just that she—all of you, you didn't have to trouble yourselves. I told you, I'll come back."

"Then, we will stand beside you until you leave."

Gary sighed, they wouldn't listen to him. They really were related, they all listened to no one but themselves. They entered the dining room and Gary was surprised to see Tess joining them for breakfast. She usually had breakfast with the other maids.

"You're all up early," Gary said, getting seated.

"Believe it or not, this wasn't planned at all. Each one of us wanted to see you out and we just bumped into each other," Uncle Charlie explained.

"Mhm, I don't believe it," Gary responded, making most of them laugh. This was meant to be breakfast? There was so much to eat. This would have counted as a buffet.

"Wow, Tess, you made all this?" Gary asked.

"I work here, I knew that everyone was going to be awake. So I thought, why not do something special. Now, are we going to eat or just talk?" Tess asked, her plate already filled with food. All the other maids would still be asleep. She must have woken up very early to be able to cook all this on her own. Everyone complimented her cooking, she was actually really good. They ate and talked all through breakfast and there still was a lot of food untouched. Tess said she'd leave it for the other maids.

"You know how to write, so you have no excuse not to write after getting there. If they train you too hard and you can't keep up, don't be shy, tell them you need to rest." Mrs. Sligmen had been fussing for a while now. They were standing outside the front door waiting for the bus to arrive. Mr. Davis, the butler, joined them outside.

"I can hear a bus nearby," Mr. Sligmen said, waving his hand for Gary to get ready.

The bus drove through the front gates, rounded the small roundabout around the water fountain, and stopped halfway, right in front of them. The door opened and the bus driver got out. He walked towards Gary to take his duffle bag, but the butler raised the duffle bag in his hand to show him that he'd put it away. The driver walked back into to the bus.

"I got to go," Gary said, turning to his family.

"Don't forget to write," Mrs. Sligmen reminded him.

"I won't forget. Goodbye!" He turned away.

"Goodbye," they all responded. Lucy and her father were waving their hands.

Gary looked for an empty spot to sit down when someone grabbed his hand. It was the high-ranked military man.

"So you're a rich boy, huh?" he said, motioning Gary to sit on the empty seat beside him.

"You could say that," Gary responded, looking at his family through the window as they drove away.

"I didn't expect that. You don't seem like a rich kid at all."

"Well, I wasn't always rich," Gary said without realizing what he was saying.

"What?" The man asked, now confused.

"Oh, um, I used to live with my parents. They didn't have much wealth," Gary explained, regretting saying anything.

"Well, what happened to them? Your parents?"

"They, uh, they left," Gary lied. He didn't mean to lie, but he couldn't bring himself to tell the truth either.

"Oh, I'm sorry."

"It's alright. It was a long time ago. Um, anyway, I never got your name?" Gary asked, trying to change the subject.

"That's right. I didn't introduce myself, did I? The name's Garner Bennett."

"Gary Alter."

The rest of the ride was mostly silent, except for when they got close to the training center. Mr. Bennett started to explain what kind of training they'd do. He also explained how Gary could skip the last few days of training, since he was already perfect at handling a gun and didn't need to learn from the beginning.

Mr. Bennett excused himself once they got off the bus and went off into the building to the left, which looked like the place they were going to stay. The building to the right looked like a big warehouse. Was that the training center? It had to be, but it seemed as if it could collapse at any moment.

They were directed to meet at the entrance of the training center after a two-hour rest in their assigned rooms. Gary got his keys and went to his room to start unpacking when he realized that there were two beds. *I have a roommate?* he thought to himself right before the door opened again. A young man entered the room and stopped when he saw Gary.

"I guess we're roomies," the young man said.

"Yah, I'm Gary by the way," Gary introduced himself, hoping the young man would do the same without him asking.

"I know, we had classes together," the young man responded. Gary stood there confused, trying to remember who this guy was. The young man closed the door, walked over to one of the beds, and dropped his bag on the floor as he sat down on the bed, facing Gary.

"I can't believe you don't remember me. I'm Anderson. I used to sit behind you?" He looked at Gary, waiting for him to remember. Anderson sighed when Gary didn't respond.

"Wow, I thought you would at least know your competition."

"Competition?" Gary asked.

"Me! I'm your competition! We always got rivaling marks. Some teachers were also betting between which of us was going to get first place at graduation," Anderson explained.

"Oh, sorry, I didn't realize. I should've paid more attention," Gary apologized.

"It's okay. To be honest, I always thought you'd surpass me. Since I'm only book-smart. I learn the book and do what it says. I'm not that good at theorizing, but you're a genius. I get why most of the teachers are on your side," Anderson mumbled as he stretched out on his bed and relaxed.

"I'm sure you're overestimating me." Gary put his duffle bag down on the other bed and started unpacking.

He didn't want to look at Anderson more than he had to. He resembled Jay too much. He had black hair and eyes, like Jay. He also had Jay's manner of speech and confidence. Gary hoped that they had made a mistake and one of them would have to move out of the room.

Two hours later, everyone was gathered at the entrance to the training center. There Mr. Bennett introduced himself and explained that he was assigned to supervise their training with another military unit, which was why he came to the meeting two weeks ago with the same exact trainee soldiers.

They entered the training center, and unlike the exterior, the interior was full of new workout machines on one side and a big open area on the other. There were some men working out using the machines, and Gary spotted Tristen among them. Mr. Bennett clapped twice loudly and all the men stopped what they were doing and stood in a line in front of Mr. Bennett, all with their hands folded behind their back.

"Each one of you will have one of these supervise your training." Mr. Bennett pointed at the men now behind him as he was explaining to Gary's group what to do.

"Choose whoever you want and start. Each person has to complete the training on the board by lunchtime. Now go, start, begin!" he said before walking away.

Gary stared at the men in front of him. Was he supposed to choose someone on his own? He'd rather get chosen than have to choose someone. He was so lost in thought that he didn't realize Tristen walking up to him.

"Hey, you're that good kid, right? Wanna partner up?" he asked.

"Alright," Gary answered.

They took turns with each set of exercises that were written on the board next to the door. Tristen was using the seated overhead press when he caught Gary looking at Anderson.

"Is he like a friend or a bully?" he asked.

"What?! No. I—I just met him. Today. He's my roommate."

"Why do you keep looking at him?"

"He just reminds me of someone I used to know," Gary answered, still staring at Anderson.

"Oh, he reminds you of a friend."

"Not a friend exactly. He was more like a, uh...never mind." Gary stopped himself before he could finish, still staring. He didn't want old memories to hold him back now. There was no time for 'him.' The entire country was falling. He had to stay strong. Gary realized that Tristen had let go of the overhead press and was staring at him.

"You okay?" he asked.

"Don't worry about it. It's just someone I used to know. We weren't close or anything," Gary replied, pulling himself together. Tristen was still staring at Gary. Gary didn't know what to do, so he kept looking back and forth between Tristen and the ground.

"Yah, okay," Tristen replied after some time, but Gary could tell that he didn't believe him.

After everyone had finished exercising, they all went back to the main building for lunch. Mr. Bennett found Gary, who was sitting with Anderson, and asked him to come back to the training center after he finished eating. Anderson decided to tag along with Gary after lunch. So they both went back to the training center together. When they got there, Mr. Bennett told them that it was shooting practice now and if they were able to completely learn it, they wouldn't have extra training hours the last three days of the week, unlike the other medical students.

Mr. Bennett said that he would only allow Gary this opportunity since Gary was already very good with guns, but after meeting Anderson, he agreed to allow him to train with Gary. It seemed that Anderson was a very likable person. Although, after the first few shots, it was clear that Anderson wasn't the best with a gun.

Chapter 11
War?

He sat down opposite Gary with two envelopes in his hand. After looking at the names on each, he passed one to Gary and looked down at the one in his hand.

"Should we open them?" Gary asked Anderson.

"I think they wouldn't have given us the envelopes if they didn't want us to open them. Don't worry though, I'm sure you passed," Anderson answered as he started tearing his envelope open. "I passed. No surprise there. I'd be surprised if I didn't pass," he said.

Gary carefully opened the envelope in his hand and read what was written on the piece of paper inside.

"I passed too," Gary said while taking a gulp of breath. He hadn't realized that he had been holding his breath. Was he doubting his ability to pass? Did he actually want to fail?

"What's your overall mark?" Anderson asked.

"Ninety-eight point nine." Gary answered.

"What?! That's exactly what I got! I thought you'd at least get ninety-nine. What happened to you? You always get the highest marks. We never got the same mark before!" Anderson was very surprised by Gary's grade.

"I'll admit, I didn't study that well for these exams. But ninety eight is still very good, considering I didn't study well." Gary folded the paper and put it back in the envelope, then got up from his bed and sat down at the table to write a letter to his family telling them he passed. Anderson was still on his bed rereading his paper.

The last Gary heard from his family was two days ago when Lucy wrote him a letter. Apparently, the virus got worse and the whole country was under quarantine. Everyone had to take safety measures when going out. There had also been an outbreak of the virus in the neighboring country and they also had to set a curfew for the all citizens and take safety measures when they left their houses. So that would mean that they were no longer at a disadvantage and had a higher chance of finding a cure to the virus first.

"Isn't it crazy?" Anderson said, lying down on his bed and staring up at the ceiling.

"What?" Gary asked.

"We're going to war tomorrow," Anderson explained. "Well, it is crazy when you put it like that."

"No, it's crazy in every way possible." Gary chuckled without realizing what he was doing.

"I'm serious! We're just boys, yet they still want us to help them win a war! Next, they'll have an army of trained monkeys to fight for them!"

"Monkeys? Are you alright? The training must have gotten to you," Gary responded.

"Haven't you got an imagination?" Anderson asked.

"Of course I do," Gary said, slightly offended.

"Well, I'm just trying to prove my point. The training was too easy to 'get to me' these past two days. It's been easier since I had the extra shooting practice with you before. I haven't thanked you for letting me join you, have I?"

"You have, actually, twice already," Gary corrected.

"Oh, maybe the training got to me just a little bit," Anderson admitted, smiling at himself.

"Are you going to stay up late?" Anderson asked Gary.

"No, I'll just finish this up and go to bed." Gary turned around to see Anderson in bed.

"Don't mind me, I won't make any noise," Gary said as he got up, turned off the lights, sat back down at the desk, and turned on the little table light.

"It's not like you can make any noise," said Anderson teasingly.

Gary took Anderson's remark as a compliment and continued writing the letter.

*

There were three buses this time. One was prepared to take the students that had failed the exams back home. The other two were to take the rest of them, both the trainee soldiers and the students that passed, to the 'war zone,' which was basically where they had set up camp.

Gary sat next to Anderson this time. Unlike when he first met him, Gary grew fond of Anderson. They were talking when Mr. Bennett and Tristan, who were sitting on the seats in front of them, turned around and joined the conversation. Mr. Bennett then asked Anderson and Gary how they knew each other.

"I know Gary for almost three years now. But it seems Gary's head is so in the clouds that he didn't know about me until last week," Anderson answered.

"How did you know about Gary if he didn't know about you?" Tristen asked.

"By our marks. We are the best students at our school, so everyone would compare us to each other and I always tried to get higher marks than Gary. There was a time when I held first place, but it wasn't for long," Anderson explained.

"Oh, so you're smart, talented, and rich, huh?" Mr. Bennett counted off.

"You're rich?" Both Tristan and Anderson asked.

"I'm not rich, my family is just very wealthy," Gary said.

"Didn't you say your family wasn't very wealthy?" Mr. Bennett asked.

"My parents aren't wealthy. I live with my grandparents, they're wealthy," Gary explained.

"Well, what happened to your parents?" Anderson asked.

Gary went quiet for a while then sighed. He couldn't lie forever.

"My mom is dead and my dad is in prison. So I moved to my grandparents' house." Everyone went quiet, staring at Gary. "It's really no big deal. It was years ago so it doesn't matter," Gary added.

"Wait, wasn't it that case, um, Gary and Jay Alter?" Mr. Bennett asked.

"Yes, it was," Gary answered, surprised that Mr. Bennett knew about him.

"I knew I had heard your name somewhere before. It was my first day at work when I heard about you two. I also watched it on the news that night. You must have been through a lot."

"What's going on? What happened?" Tristen asked.

"You shouldn't ask," Mr. Bennett stopped him.

"It's alright, really. I've gotten over it," Gary explained.

"Well then, what happened?" Anderson asked.

"It started when my brother ran away from home. My parents got angry about it. They kept fighting over whose fault it was. My dad lost his temper one day and killed my mom. So he was sent to prison and I moved to my grandparents' house."

"Wow, your life is full of drama," Anderson said, looking at Gary with wide eyes.

"What happened to your brother?" Tristen asked.

"They never found him. He's considered dead," Gary replied.

"Why did your brother run away?" Mr. Bennett asked.

"No one really knows why. They think it might be because our parents were abusive. But I don't believe that."

"Your parents were abusive?" Tristen asked unbelievingly.

"It just keeps getting worse," Anderson added.

"Why did he run away?" Mr. Bennett asked.

"I'm not sure. I only remember him telling me it was bigger than life or death, but that's all he said," Gary explained.

"If he said that, then it must have been because of your parents, don't you think so?" Anderson concluded.

"I don't know," Gary said.

"You were six when it happened, right?" Mr. Bennett asked.

"Yeah," Gary answered.

"Sir, we've reached the camp." They were interrupted by a soldier that sat a few seats behind them.

They all looked out the window and saw gray and black camps everywhere. There was one very big white tent in the middle, which Gary guessed was the medical tent.

Mr. Bennett stood up and addressed everyone, saying that they were to leave in a straight line when they got off and wait for orders.

"Hey, it's going to be okay. Don't think about it too much," Anderson said to Gary in an attempt to be empathetic.

"Alright," responded Gary. Did he seriously just say 'it's going to be okay'? How could he judge when he hadn't gone through the same thing himself? That was just rude and invalidated all that Gary went through and all his feelings. It made him feel weak for knowing that it wasn't 'okay' and it would never be 'okay.' Anderson just didn't understand that.

After they got off the bus, Gary and the other doctors were directed to go to the long tent beside the big white one, which was a medical tent. The long black tent was the one they were going to be sleeping in. The soldiers, on the other hand, were told to find a tent to stay in all by themselves.

Gary chose a bed that was between two occupied beds on purpose. He didn't feel like talking to Anderson. Gary was about to start unpacking when a young woman wearing a medical uniform stepped in the tent and started talking, addressing everyone that was there.

"Looks like all of you are here. If you all gather up so I can tell you some stuff, that would be great," she said. After everyone got closer, she continued. "Okay. First of all, my name's Zoya and I'm in charge of all things medical here. I expect you all have your own medical bags?" she asked. Everyone including Gary nodded.

"Good, you'll be needing those for when you go out on the field. Now, don't get nervous. Only a few go out on the field and only after the fight ends and enemy soldiers have retreated. We can't really go out if it's not safe. After you finish unpacking here, come over to the medical tent. Just walk around, memorize where the medicine is kept, get to know where we treat patients with long-term recovery and where we treat patients with emergency-level injuries. If you get to know some of the other doctors, that would be good, too. If you find any work you can help in, don't hesitate to volunteer. So, that's it. If you have any questions, come find me." Zoya nodded her head before leaving the same way she came.

After Gary unpacked, he turned to see Anderson waiting for him. Gary felt a little guilty for getting angry at him before. Besides, it wasn't his fault, almost everyone made the same mistake after the incident with his family. He silently agreed to look around together. It was as if they walked out into a schoolyard as soon as they walked out of the tent. There were people running around, some playing games and some exercising, while others were playing cards or just chatting.

"I didn't expect this when they said war," Gary said.

"Well, what did you expect?" Anderson asked.

"It's stupid, but I thought everyone would be serious, gloomy, and miserable," Gary answered.

"I take it back, you definitely have a wild imagination," Anderson replied.

Almost a month passed by when Fred came along. He had been in the military before college so it wasn't surprising to see him there. The group that Fred had come with had two people that had caught the virus, so as soon as Fred's group arrived, they all had to be tested and quarantined until they were confirmed to be virus-free. Fortunately, Fred tested negative to the virus and was out of quarantine in a few hours.

"So, Gary, the person who's always alone, finally has a friend?" Fred asked while watching Gary fill out some documents regarding his patients.

"What?" Gary responded.

"You and that black-haired guy are always together."

"Oh, you mean Anderson. He's the only person I know here, so it's easier to be around him than anyone else."

"You know, he does remind me of someone," Fred added.

"Jay?" Gary said, without taking his eyes off of the paper.

"Is that why you chose him?"

"Fred, I'm sorry, but I'm really busy right now. Can't this wait?" Gary finally looked up.

"Okay, I'm sorry. I'll leave you alone. But don't forget to introduce me to him later," Fred said before leaving.

After Gary finished his work for that day, he helped Anderson finish what was left of his work, then told him that someone wanted to meet him. They walked over to the tent that Fred was staying in. Fred was sitting outside the tent with some others, talking. When he saw Gary, he got up and walked over to them.

"Anderson, this this Fred. Fred, Anderson," Gary introduced.

"Hey," Anderson said, looking at Fred.

"Hi, Anderson. I have a question for you. Why Gary?" Fred asked.

"Hey!" Gary said to Fred.

"Well, we were roommates a few weeks back and I want to see how he's so smart," Anderson explained.

"So it's because he's smart?"

"Yah, I've always tried to surpass him, but he's better than me when it comes to working from scratch. That's what a doctor has to perfect to be a good doctor."

"Again, you're overestimating me," Gary added.

"Hey, you made another friend without me?" Tristen said, joining their group.

"Hi, I'm Fred. Gary's friend." Fred held his hand out towards Tristen.

"I'm Tristen."

Chapter 12
Kidnapping

Gary and Anderson just finished with their shift. It was after sunset and they were going to rest when Zoya spotted them. It was a busy day and there was a battle raging, so there were a lot of people being brought in with injuries. Zoya told them that the battle was over and they had secured the area where the fight occurred. They needed people to scout the area and help the injured. Anderson and Gary agreed to go.

They first went to get their sling first-aid bags. Gary got his bag and started checking that he had everything when he found the three small glass bottles that had the extra serum from his graduation project.

"What is that?" Anderson asked.

"It's from my graduation project. I forgot I put it here," Gary replied.

"Oh, you scared me. I thought I didn't have everything. Well, just leave it where you found it. That way it won't get mixed up with the other bottles."

"Okay. Alright."

Gary and Anderson went out to see Fred and Tristen waiting for them next to the truck that was to take them to the battleground.

"What are you two doing here?" Gary asked.

"Every time doctors go out, they have to have a soldier to help and guard them. We heard from the general that you guys were going and we thought, why not?" Fred answered.

"The general?" Anderson asked.

"Mr. Bennett." Tristen answered.

"If he's the general, then why did he train us?" Anderson questioned.

"He saw Gary's skills." Tristen said, "Oh."

They climbed into the back of the truck and in a few minutes, they arrived at a small village. The houses were destroyed, the roofs had caved in on each house, and debris was everywhere. There were houses with only half a wall standing, all the windows were broken, doors were unhinged, bashed in, and broken. Overall, it was a complete mess. Gary and the others got off of the truck one by one after they stopped in front of the village.

"Here, put these on, you two," Fred said, handing Gary and Anderson each a belt. Each belt had a gun strapped onto it with a small sachet of ammo on the other side.

"Why? We have you guys." Anderson said, holding his belt.

"Extra precautionary measures," Tristen answered.

"They don't even blend in with our clothes," Anderson added.

"Of course not, you wear white," Fred pointed out.

"Just put it on," Gary told Anderson, his belt already around his waist. It was a little big, so the gun fell to the side, but it wasn't big enough to fall to the ground.

They walked towards the houses, looking around. There were bodies here and there, some enemy soldiers, some allies. Gary felt guilty for being able to do nothing more than look. In some weird way, everything he saw in front of him felt like it happened because of his ignorance and incapability to do anything.

Gary felt a pain in his chest that centered around his heart. Was this what emotions are capable of doing to a person? It felt like someone had lit a fire inside of him and it was warm, but not a good warm. His eyes felt hot, he felt like crying, but how could he cry while everyone else was composed? *I need to say sorry, I have to apologize to them!* Gary thought to himself.

"Look at this." Tristen was kneeling next to a corpse hidden to the side of a building. They walked over to him.

"Shot in the head. But if you look closer, you can see burn marks." Tristen analyzed, pointing at the bloody mess on the man's head.

"Suicide," Gary said.

"It was an enemy soldier," Fred added, pointing at a badge on the man's chest. It was a black snake with green eyes, twisted into an infinity.

"He must have been scared. I don't blame him," Anderson said.

"Come on. We don't have much time. Let's move on," Fred explained.

They walked deeper into the village. As Gary looked around, he realized that if this place was fixed up, it would have resembled the neighborhood he lived in when he was young. Something suddenly made Gary stop in his tracks. There was a faint sound of whining.

"What's wrong?" Anderson asked Gary.

"I hear something. This way," he said, walking towards the sound. It was a dog stuck underneath some debris. Fred ran towards it and started to dig it out from beneath the debris. They all started to move debris aside and in a few seconds the dog was free. It stood there for a while, then started walking away.

"Wait, hold it down. Don't let it get away," Gary instructed, getting up.

"Why?" Tristen asked, rushing into action.

"It has a deep wound. It could cause an infection," Gary explained as Tristen and Fred caught the dog and held it down. The dog tried to shake them off but they had a strong hold on it.

"You'd even go all the way to help a dog during a war?" Anderson admired.

"After you get to know him, you'd learn that he can't hurt a fly without feeling bad about it," Fred expressed.

"Fred. Come on, that's not true," Gary said. He liked being praised and complimented, but he hated being in the spotlight and the center of attention.

"There. That should be enough," Gary said. The wound was on the dog's side. Gary had cleaned it, added some ointment, and wrapped it up. They let the dog go and it walked away in a hurry. They got up and continued walking when they ended up on the outer edge of the village. There were houses on one side and trees on the other.

"Hey, over here! Here!" someone said, waving their hand. It was a mid-aged man leaning against the wall of a house. The four of them rushed over to help.

"Are you alright?" Anderson said as he and Gary scanned the man.

"I'm okay, but my friend back there couldn't move. I thought I could get help, but I couldn't get far with my leg," the man said, looking to his left.

"We'll go get the other guy. You two stay here and help him," Fred said, looking at Tristen and Gary. Anderson and Fred walked off in the direction the man said to go.

There was blood on the man's pants. It seemed he had been shot in the upper thigh. Gary opened his first-aid bag and started getting ready to clean the wound when it all happened.

There was a big bang and Gary saw Tristen fall to the ground beside him. He was bleeding from his head. It looked like the bullet came from the trees behind him. Gary felt his heart beating fast. Still crouching down, he scooted over to block the man from whomever was hidden in the trees.

"Stay in front of me," Gary instructed when the man reached out, grabbed Gary's gun and pointed it towards Gary's head.

"Get up. Now, quick!" The man stood up with ease. Was he even hurt? Why was he pointing the gun at Gary? Was he confused? Either way, Gary was too petrified to think. He got up slowly, the sling bag on his stomach wide open.

"Close the bag! Close it!" the man instructed.

Gary zipped up the bag and raised his hands up again. "Walk towards the trees! Turn around and walk!" the man shouted. Gary did as he was told, getting more nervous by the second. They passed the tree line when Gary saw another man holding a big gun in his hands.

"Wait here. The other two are coming back," the man holding the big gun said. After a while, Anderson and Fred came running back to where Tristen was lying on the ground. Anderson kneeled down next to Tristen. After a few seconds, Gary heard Anderson saying there was no pulse. Tristen…was dead?

The man holding the big gun aimed it at Fred. Gary was about to move when he felt cold metal on the back of his head.

"Don't even think about it." The man said, aiming the gun at Gary.

"Gary!" Fred and Anderson started shouting, looking for Gary. Anderson moved and stood in front of Fred, blocking him from view as he looked around.

"Move out of the way," Gary heard the man whisper, still aiming the gun.

Anderson turned towards Fred. It looked like they were talking. They started walking back the way they all came from before the man had called them over, calling Gary's name. Anderson was still blocking Fred.

"Ugh, let's just go," the man said, lowering the big gun to his side.

"What? What about the other one?" the man behind Gary asked.

"We have one, and if I shoot the guy now, the other one will just run away," the other man responded.

"Fine then."

They walked deeper into the woods. The trees got bigger and wider then started to get smaller and thinner. Soon they were out in the open again. There was a car waiting there for them. They got in the back with Gary in the middle and there was already a driver in the front, who teased the other men for only being able to get one doctor.

Gary was panicking. He felt as if all the muscles in his body were tensing up and relaxing very fast. His muscles ached and he thought he was trembling, but when he looked down at his hands, he was completely steady.

He inhaled but couldn't get the satisfaction of a fresh breath of air. He felt suffocated. He couldn't breathe yet; he still struggled to keep his breath silent and steady.

So many thoughts rushed through his head. He didn't know if he was in control of his own thoughts anymore. He couldn't tell what he was thinking, let alone if he was thinking at all. His head rushed with so many thoughts and his head ached so much, it was a surprise there was room for all his thoughts.

Gary could hear everything around him just fine but it wasn't the only thing he heard. He also heard a ringing that hurt his ears. This horrible ringing would make anyone reach up and try to protect their ears by covering them. Instead, Gary kept his hands on his lap and waited it out.

His eyes were playing tricks on him. He'd see clearly one second and he couldn't see at all the next. He felt as if the world was revolving around him. He didn't know if he was sitting up straight or if he was leaning to the side.

Gary felt the urge to scream. Just scream. But he couldn't. Not because there were people around him, but because he didn't know how to scream. He knew how a person would scream, but he himself didn't know if he could scream anymore.

All in all, Gary felt weird. How he felt couldn't simply be explained for a person to understand, it had to be experienced. The last he felt this way was the last time he saw his mother. He couldn't control himself afterwards that time. He didn't want to lose control again. He couldn't lose control.

Gary looked up. They were getting close to what looked like a big building surrounded by tents of all shapes and sizes.

"You see that big building in the middle?" the man to Gary's right asked. He was the same guy who shot Tristen.

Gary didn't respond.

"You'll be working there from now on," the man continued.

"What makes you think I'll work for you after you killed my friend?" Gary said in a low but firm voice.

"This is war. Anyone could die here. We don't get to choose who lives and who dies. Besides, there's one of you and thousands of us. Who do you think'll win in a fight?" the driver explained.

"The other doctor is doing his job, so what makes you any different?" the man on Gary's left added. Other doctor? What other doctor? Had they taken someone else before?

They drove all the way to the side of the big building, where there was an entrance of big double doors. They got out of the car and walked in where a room, twice as big as the kitchen back at Gary's home, was filled with rows of beds. Some had patients lying down and some were empty. There were a few doctors here and there taking care of the patients. The room was dimly lit by a few lamps beside some of the beds. The man that drove them here walked up to one of the doctors and called him over.

"Another one?! I swear, you three are going to get in trouble one of these days!" the doctor whispered fiercely when he spotted Gary.

"Yah. Like that's ever going to happen," the same man said.

Chapter 13
Adjusting

The three men, after being told off by the doctor, left Gary with him and said they were going to bed. The doctor gave Gary a quick tour, showing him the two emergency surgical rooms, the medical storage room, the room that housed the heavily injured, and the room that held the lightly injured and ill, which was also the room Gary first entered through.

The doctor took Gary to a small kitchen with little tables and chairs, where he asked if Gary wanted anything to eat. Gary declined, saying that he wasn't hungry. He stuttered while saying that, but he couldn't help it; he was nervous. The doctor reached his hand towards Gary. What did he want? Gary didn't know what he was supposed to do. The doctor had locked eyes with Gary. The doctor was still waiting with his hand out. Gary felt as if he had to do something, so he reached out and shook the doctor's hand. The doctor didn't let go.

"You're sweating," the doctor said, letting go of Gary's hand.

"W-what?" Gary asked.

"You're sweating, you're stuttering, and I can hear you breathing unevenly," the doctor explained.

Gary didn't respond.

"You should calm down. Here, sit," the doctor said, pulling a chair.

Gary sat down.

"I studied mental health when I was younger. The way you're acting and your physical symptoms tell me that you are very nervous. I can't really diagnose you right now. But I wouldn't be surprised if you are having a panic attack. I'm sorry if I seem selfish, but I don't have time for this. Calm yourself down. We're not going to kill you. The reason they brought you here was because after the epidemic spread to our country, we needed more doctors to help. We don't actually have many doctors here, so they pulled the doctors from the army, which wasn't the best choice, but what else could they do?" the doctor continued.

Were they really in that bad of a situation? Gary felt guilty for believing them to be the villains.

"My name is Miles Miller. If you ever feel uncomfortable or have any questions about anything, find me and I won't ignore you. Just remember that."

Now that Gary had calmed down, he realized how gentle Miller's brown eyes were. Miller had rough black skin and frizzy short black hair. The dim lights and Miller's wrinkly old face would have scared Gary back in the day. However, Miller's brown eyes, like the leaves of a brown willow tree, had such a gentle and bright color that redefined the word 'magnificent.'

Gary drank some water from the bottle that Miller had given him. This calmed him down the most. The water was just the right amount of cold and even though it tasted different, it didn't taste bad at all.

"So I'm going to ask you about yourself now. Can you tell me who you are and what type of doctor you are?" Miller asked.

"I'm—my name is Gary and I'm a surgeon. I focus mainly on diagnosing people, performing surgeries, uh...f-for both diseases and injuries and I keep track of their healing," Gary explained.

"Good. We need surgeons. So I guess I'll put you in the emergency room. Do you know how to work with bullet wounds?" Miller added.

"Yes. I can work with many injuries, even if the weapon is still in the body," Gary assured.

"So I'll let you get some rest for tonight and I'll introduce you to everyone tomorrow," Miller concluded.

Miller took Gary to a room where everyone was asleep on bunk beds. He showed Gary to a free bed, where Gary put his sling bag before going to the bathroom to wash up before bed. Miller also gave him a change of clothes.

As Gary lay down on his bed, listening to everyone's heavy breaths, he felt guilt build up inside of him. He just witnessed one of his friend's death, yet he hadn't shed a single tear. Was he really a good person? Gary didn't believe he was. Now that he thought about it, he hadn't cried since he was young. If he tried to cry right there, would he be able to? He wanted to cry, but he couldn't.

The next day Miller introduced Gary to the people who worked in the emergency surgical rooms and to Haden. Apparently, Haden was also abducted like Gary. He had been there for a couple of weeks now, so he was able to tell Gary that the people there weren't anything to be afraid of.

Thereafter, Gary was bombarded with work. Whenever Gary had some time off, it would be to eat, use the bathroom, or to sleep at night. He couldn't write letters to his family now, but that wasn't important at the moment. He had to focus on his work.

A week later, the same three men that had kidnapped Gary came to visit. They weren't as scary as Gary thought; they were just very cheeky and cunning. It turned out, they had gone out to get some more doctors, but it seemed, after losing Gary and Haden, they stopped sending doctors out. Instead, they just sent out some soldiers who had been trained with first aid.

After a while, rumors started to spread about a soldier who had come with the new batch of soldiers. They said he was strong and had many years of experience since he had been training since he was young. People also said that he was the son of one of the top military personnel in the government, so most of them knew him.

Chapter 14
Unbelievable

Gary was working with Hazel, a doctor, and Tom, a nurse. The person they were working on had torn the anterior cruciate ligament and broken their kneecap. It was a Grade 3 injury. He had jumped from up high to evade fire when he injured his knee. It was so bad that even with surgery, proper mobility wasn't guaranteed.

They were almost done now. All that was left was to stitch the guy up. It was quiet. Then there was a knock on the door and Tom went to see who it was. A few minutes later Tom came back in and Hazel had finished with the stitches.

"Finally! My hands are aching," Hazel sighed. She had been working for a while now. Gary and Hazel had been taking turns with each surgery, but Hazel had been working before Gary's shift started.

"Hey, guys, they need a doctor out there. Someone's been shot and is in critical condition, you should go see," Tom said, moving in to finish up while Hazel and Gary went to see what was going on.

"What's wrong?" Hazel asked Floyd, the doctor that usually worked in the other emergency room.

"There's someone who's been shot. By the looks of it, the bullet must have pierced the heart. Look, I know I'm the oldest here, but I don't know how to work with something like that," Floyd responded.

"You two rest. I'll do this one," Gary said. He knew what to do in case the heart was hit. He just hoped it wasn't too bad. Gary went into the other emergency room and asked Anthony, the nurse, to get things ready.

The guy that was lying on the bed looked young, he wasn't very tall. His black hair covered his eyes and he was breathing heavily. Gary lifted the man's hair up and put his hand on the man's forehead. He was heating up. Gary looked at the man's face and he froze.

The man was looking back at Gary. A delicate, soft blue eye and a black staring at Gary. What? *Who is this? Jay? It can't be! Jay is dead! I'm hallucinating! This can't be Jay, can it? Why is he staring at me? But this man's right eye is the black one, Jay's eyes are the opposite, aren't they? Wait, are they? I don't remember!*

"Gary, are you alright?" Anthony asked, snapping Gary out of his trance.

"Yes, but...this guy is still awake," Gary said.

Anthony knew what Gary meant and went to get the anesthetics. Gary tried to focus on anything else. Anything.

Anthony had everything ready now. Gary sanitized everything and cleaned the wound, then cut a small incision. After looking into things, both Gary and Anthony were surprised to see that the bullet didn't penetrate the heart, but instead it had hit one of the ribs. The rib had broken, but fortunately it was a clean break, so it would heal on its own in about six weeks. The broken rib hadn't pierced anything either. All that Gary had to do was take out the bullet and clean out the wound to make sure infections wouldn't spread. After a while, Gary was done with the surgery.

"Can you finish things up here?" Gary asked Anthony.

"I was going to tell you to go and rest. You were trembling the whole time," Anthony responded.

"Thank you," Gary was about to leave when he felt his heart beat once very fiercely. Like a mini heart attack.

"Is the blood transfusion okay?!" Gary asked Anthony in his panic.

"Yes! It's okay. I checked on it twice. You scared me…" Anthony answered.

"Oh, sorry," Gary said as he left. Why was he so concerned? Even if it was Jay, Gary had already decided that he hated Jay and that he'd moved on. He didn't care.

Gary went to bed early that night but only got close to three hours of sleep. He couldn't stop thinking about having to meet 'that' man and talk to him the next day. He could only hope that when he read the report, Jay's name wouldn't be on the front page.

The next day, Gary got up reluctantly and ate breakfast with some others in the kitchen. Afterwards, Gary had to check with all the patients that he had treated that were still recovering. He would ask them some questions and explain what was going to happen with their recovery now.

Each patient had their own report on the table next to their bed. There weren't many people in this room since it held the heavily injured. So Gary could clearly see the man he worked on last night lying on one of the beds across the room. Miller was talking to that man. Did they know each other? Miller looked concerned for the man, but the man was happily waving him off. It looked like something was going on and the man didn't want Miller to worry about it.

Miller walked away as Gary finished with his last patient before that man. Gary walked over to the man and reached for the report on the table. The man was looking at Gary through his hair. The man's hair was long enough to cover his left eye, hiding it from sight, but if a person were to focus, they would be able to see the blue color. Gary looked down at the report and analyzed the first page. Gary held his breath when he read the name: Jay… Gary skipped the first page and read on.

"Jay Alter. You've been shot in the chest. None of your organs have been—" Gary started. He was trying not to look up from the report when he was interrupted.

"Gary. Another doctor already told me everything," Jay said. His voice had matured a lot.

"Then, I'll have to ask you some questions," Gary said, turning the pages to the question page.

"He did that too," Jay responded. He was right. Gary saw the answers written on the page.

"Gary. Come on, we finally see each other again and this is how you act?" Jay asked.

"I don't know what you are trying to say," Gary said, trying to pretend he didn't know who Jay was.

"I know that's not true. You just said my name."

"I read your name off of the front page."

"Read it again."

Gary flipped back to the front page and read the name again. Jay. That was it. Jay.

"You said Jay Alter. My name is Jay. Just Jay," Jay explained.

Gary stayed quiet.

"How did you get here?" Jay asked.

"I could ask you the same thing," Gary said, finally looking at Jay.

"Hey, I didn't plan this," Jay responded.

"But you planned your escape," Gary said.

"I was a kid. I didn't know anything."

"I was a kid too, but you still left me alone."

"Gary, I'm sorry."

"Sorry isn't going to change anything. In fact, your apology is about twenty years too late," Gary's voice was full of anger and hate, but he tried not to shout as not to disturb anyone.

"If you would just listen to me, I could explain everything," Jay pleaded.

"No. I'm not going to listen to you. You became a stranger to me the day you jumped out of the window, and with the whole war going on, I have bigger problems. So I'd like it if you didn't act as if you knew me," Gary replied.

"But I do know you."

"Really? Then you must know which college I went to since I graduated not too long ago."

"Gary. I don't know that, but—"

"But nothing," Gary said.

"What's going on here?" It was a soldier. He seemed to know Jay. Did he come to visit him?

"Nothing," Gary said to the soldier as he put the report back on the table and walked away.

Gary felt guilty for fighting with Jay, but he had so many emotions swirling inside of him, he didn't know which to listen to. So, naturally, the emotions that ended up controlling him was anger and rage. It was as if the only way Gary could cope with everything that was happening was to rage at the people he loved the most. Wait, loved? He thought he hated Jay. So why did he think that he loved him? He didn't love Jay. He hated him.

When Gary talked to Jay, it seemed like Jay was trying to go back to the way they were before. Did Jay care about Gary? Did he regret running away and leaving Gary to deal with their parents alone? Or was Jay just pretending? Was he trying to get on Gary's good side for if he needed Gary in the future? Or did he really miss Gary as much as Gary missed him? Did Gary actually miss him? Did they miss each other?